THE WOLF INSIDE US

DARIAN HART

The Wolf Inside us
Darian Hart

© 2022 Oxford eBooks Ltd.
Published under the sci-fi-cafe.com imprint.
www.oxford-ebooks.com

This is a work of fiction. All the characters and events
portrayed in this book are products of the writer's imagination,
or are used fictitiously.
Respect is given to the creators of any works mentioned in this book
or where inspiration has been drawn.

ISBN 978-1-910779-97-2 (Paperback)

sci-fi-cafe.com

CHAPTER 1

EVERY TIME KAT came to this part of town, she felt a tiny pang of envy. This was the *nice* part of town, the expensive part where doctors and architects lived. This was the place where people sat in the sunshine outside little hipster cafes, drinking little cups of coffee grown by happy families on some mountain where jaguars roamed wild and free... It would be nice if it wasn't for the bloody hipsters.

It was a Friday and the early March sun was doing its best to create a pleasant afternoon and Kat could *really* do with a proper coffee.

Rounding the corner, she came to the place she needed to be. The outer façade of the recently built apartment block was finished in Georgian style stone blocks to blend with the older parts of town. It was probably designed by one of the architects that lived up the road in one of those million-pound town houses with the little wrought-iron balconies that nobody ever used.

The keypad beeped quietly as she entered her entrance code, then dutifully, the outer door to the apartment block unlatched with a *thunk*.

The entrance lobby was probably larger than the whole of her own apartment and served no practical purpose that Kat could determine. The fully mirrored far wall made it look even larger and brought more light into the space. She took a lift to the top floor – there were two sets of lifts; she enjoyed the sheer opulence of the whole thing, like being in a fancy hotel. She should live in a place like this. Maybe one day.

Jake's apartment was at the end of the hall. It was lined with doors to the other, seemingly smaller apartments. Smaller, but nonetheless still far outside of her own budget.

She pushed the doorbell, and waited. No sound, but that wasn't unusual. Once more, and no reply. Kat sighed and reached into her pocket for her keys, selected a chrome one with one of those red rubber covers on it and opened the door.

"Jake? I'm coming in," she called around the door, "you'd better be decent!" she added, joking. Actually, no not joking; she'd come into the apartment a couple of weeks ago to find him standing motionless in the middle of the living room wearing just his underpants and a VR headset.

Inside, the apartment was sparsely but tastefully furnished. Neat. Not a thing out of place. Near to the full height window Jake was at his desk, headphones on, engrossed in his work at the large drawing board.

"Hey, Jake. It's only me." She walked across the room to him and put a hand on his shoulder. He jumped and his headphones fell off into his lap.

"Kat... Sorry, I didn't hear you come in. Lost track of time."

"No problem. Is that this week's drawings?" She pointed to the leather portfolio leaning against the couch.

"Uh, yeah. All done." Jake had returned to inking-in a panel on his drawing board.

"You know, Jerome is still happy to pay for a digital board for you. No need for me to come over each week." She *said* that, but truthfully, she enjoyed the Friday afternoon trips to pick up Jake's artwork. Firstly, she could leave work a little earlier, and secondly she would be the first to be able to read this week's episode.

When she first got the job at Inkredible Publications, the prospect of working with or even just working at the same company that published *THE* Jake Mayer's graphic novels was fantastically exciting. She had read *The Rising Flesh* since the very first edition and was one of the series' biggest fans. Though, she had to admit that she wasn't entirely thrilled by his other, more commercial work.

Sitting at the heavy marble-topped coffee table, Kat unzipped the portfolio with the reverence reserved for a holy work of art. Jake stopped drawing for a moment to assess Kat's reaction to the unfolding storyline.

After a couple of minutes, Kat wailed in anguish. "What!? Seriously, you can't kill off Michelle! What are you doing?" Before her, in bold black ink, a fist-fight with Michelle's arch enemy raged up on the roof of a decaying train carriage while the dead clawed and slavered at the sides. A lucky swipe sent the hero that readers had been rooting for from the very first episode over the edge and out of the frame. The final page depicted her demise in gruesome detail.

"How can you *do* that? You'll have the fans up in

arms about this – did you talk this through with Jerome? He's going to be pissed." She was actually shaking now, but laid the oversized page down onto the others with care.

The grin on Jake's face widened. He'd wanted to see how she would react to this cliff-hanger; she was always the first to see each issue and he truly valued her judgement. "Up in arms, huh? That's good."

"How?" she spat.

"Well, it'll get everyone talking, it'll be all over social media. And no, I didn't tell Jerome – but he's going to love it."

"Well, at least you've saved it until now. If you'd done that earlier, that offal piñata from the last frame would be *you* at the comic-con tomorrow." She paused, composed herself, she still had a job to do. "So, are you all set for tomorrow?"

Jake sighed. "I suppose. I just wish Jerome wouldn't *make* me go to these things." He laid his pen down carefully on the desk, pushed it straight and parallel with the others.

"I know, Jake" Kat got up from the couch and laid her hand on his shoulder. He flinched a little, but quickly relaxed. She spoke softly, "I know this is difficult for you, I really do. But I'll be with you, like we talked about."

"Thanks Kat," He turned his tall draughtsman's chair around to face her, more or less eye-to-eye "I'd be totally stuffed without you." For a fraction of a second, his dark brown eyes made contact with hers, then darted away.

"That's okay." She straightened, pulled her phone

out of her pocket and tapped a couple of times "So, I'll be here at seven thirty, ten minutes walk to the train station, to get the seven-fifty to London. All being well, we ought to be at Earl's Court for ten-ish. I've booked a taxi, so we can avoid the tube. Punters will be queueing for photos and signings at ten thirty." Then, looking over the top of her screen, "You figured out what you're wearing tomorrow?" eyes, dropping involuntarily to his grey sweat-pants and Manga t-shirt.

"Yes, mum." He was smiling now, feeling more relaxed knowing that Kat had all his 'outdoors' things planned.

"Cheeky git!" she chuckled, turned and began carefully shuffling the artwork in the portfolio and zipped it closed. "See you in the morning then."

And she was gone with a gentle 'snick' of the door latch. The apartment was suddenly deathly quiet. He looked out through the window at the gathering gloom outside. The evenings were starting to get lighter, and the clear, cloudless sky prolonged the darkness a little.

Jake rubbed the bridge of his nose. That headache had been building all day long now and it wasn't letting up.

The intercom chimed, he looked up. Had Kat forgotten something? He padded over to the screen embedded into the wall in the hallway – it was the supermarket delivery he'd ordered earlier that day; he'd forgotten that they were due. Jake tapped the speak icon and told the guy to leave the bags inside the lobby then buzzed the outside door open. The delivery guy looked a little confused but placed the three bags of groceries down by one of the couches in the marble-floored lobby. He paused to take it in, shrugged and left. A few seconds later, Kat came out from the lift and left the building.

When he was sure that the man had gone, Jake took the lift down and collected his shopping.

The door to Kat's apartment was still sticking and she had to bump it with her backside to get in. There were a few letters on the mat, which she stepped over; to hell with bills, it's Friday, she could sort them out on Sunday or something.

Dinner. Thank God for discount frozen food outlets. It wasn't that Kat couldn't cook for herself, but there are just times when the effort was simply too much. Nearly half the small freezer was packed with ready meals for one. All freshly made at the factory with the 'best ingredients'. These were the premium range fare, none of your one-pound frozen junk, some of these were at least two quid each.

Something French sounding went into the microwave then she flopped down on the couch.

At that moment, her phone chimed. Rolling over to pull the phone from her back pocket, she tapped on the chat group where 16 notifications were waiting for her.

<The Gurls> group were readying themselves for Friday night and they *demanded* that she come along.

[KAT] Where are we at tonight?

She typed.

Instantly, two of her friends replied that they would

be hitting the bars down Park Street in about half an hour. Okay, that sounded good but she made her excuses that she'd only come along for a couple of drinks because she had an early start in the morning.

The microwave hadn't finished yet, but Kat didn't want to get drawn into *that* conversation again. Her friends knew that she went round to Jake's every Friday, but they couldn't grasp that it was for work, and they certainly didn't appreciate the work he did.

She lay on the sofa, looking up at the slightly grubby Artex while her dinner hummed away in the little kitchen. Her friends had been making a lot of fuss over her not having a boyfriend, and joked about what they got up to in his 'fancy bachelor pad'. Of course, there was nothing at all going on... but was there a moment this afternoon when–

The microwave beeped loudly bringing her train of thought to a jarring halt.

It was a little after ten, when Kat was forced to put her phone on mute. Cries of 'Wuss', 'Lightweight' and so on had been pinging in her back pocket from the friends she left at the bar.

She pulled her coat a little tighter against a light, but cold, breeze blowing across the park and smiled at the older guy who passed by with his dog. It stopped, sniffing the air as she got underway and the man dragged the dog onwards, muttering.

A little way ahead, a wide footbridge spanned the banks and the canal in between. The bright, lampposts of the path gave way to little downlights along the railings of the bridge.

Kat glanced upwards and stopped with a little gasp. Away from the tall lampposts, the dark of the sky was clearly visible. The moonless sky was ablaze with stars, crisp and clear in the cold night air.

To the left, where she had come from, she could just about make out the top of Jake's building, just one block away from the fashionable and bustling night life that Jake would not, *could not* ever dare to enter. To her right, across the other side of the park if the lighting was better, she might have been able to see the spire of the boarded-up church at the end of the road where she lived. Two different worlds, two very different people.

A shriek from below startled her, then raucous laughter broke out from an unseen group of kids messing about under the bridge. A can clattered along the towpath followed shortly by the hiss of another being opened. The group became quieter and a familiar aroma drifted up over the edge of the bridge.

Kat scoffed quietly, and continued on her way home, across the bridge.

CHAPTER 2

Saturday 13-March 2021.

Moonrise: 06:53. Set: 18:01. 0.2%
Sunset: 18:06.

DESPITE THE BILLOWING steam, Jake was able to survey himself clearly in the large, heated bathroom mirror.

A luxurious, fluffy white towel draped over his shoulders. He wiped water from his eyes and peered at his reflection. He sucked in the beginnings of a belly, held it and let it out with a sigh.

For all the good the well-equipped gym in the basement would have done him, it was useless if he simply couldn't bear to take the lift down for fear of meeting a neighbour. The futility of having to exchange banal pleasantries made his flesh crawl.

He tried a 'strongman' pose just for fun – *shit, who am I kidding? Totally unremarkable.* He looked down, past the little birth mark under his belly button and his shoulders sagged. *Totally unremarkable.*

That headache still hadn't left him, and now it stabbed at the back of his head.

"Agh. What the hell is this?" He pushed the heels of his palms into his temples and squeezed his eyes shut against the pain.

Kat screamed in frustration, silenced the alarm on her phone and threw herself out of bed.

"Shit, shit shit... You bloody idiot Kat." Pyjamas sailed across the bedroom onto the back of a chair. They found good company with a pile of other discarded laundry. Hopping about, hurriedly getting dressed, Kat cursed herself again for setting the wrong time on her phone alarm. Seven am, just about enough time though.

"Five minutes, dress, five minutes breakfast, ten minutes across the park, couple more to Jake's..." She hovered on one foot for a moment's contemplation "Okay, just enough time to shower then." She flapped the jeans off her legs, underwear tangled somewhere within and trotted to the small, dingy bathroom.

On the way in, she grabbed a toothbrush and toothpaste, squeezing too much on then threw the tube roughly at the sink – a lucky shot, it landed inside.

No hot water, "fuuuck, fufffk, fkkkk" swearing and brushing her teeth at the same time saved valuable seconds.

A couple of minutes later, flustered but smelling like a civilised human being... well, lychee and something or other mixed with spearmint profanities just about passed muster.

Further hasty oaths convinced the impossible knot of underwear and jeans to resolve themselves, yesterday's bra was good to go and a random Zombie t-shirt completed the perfect 'don't really give a fuck, I'm just gonna hang out at the comic-con' ensemble.

The milk that actually made it into the bowl of Rice Krispies was *just about* okay and was devoured with great dexterity while managing socks and trainers.

Kat's true nature as a highly organised human being

was encompassed in the little *Rising Flesh* rucksack containing everything that she and Jake needed for their day. Train snacks, water bottle, tickets, exhibition passes – good to go, and that was it, she was out of there, down the stairs and into the street. Seven fourteen am. She grinned, yep, she was good.

"Oh, bollocks! Deodorant!" Screw it, she'd nick some of Jake's.

The elevator chimed, and the doors slid smoothly open. Darting in, Kat almost collided with a large, gentleman in shorts and vest on his way back up from the gym. They shared an awkward ride upwards, his prissy moustache twitching in distaste at the young woman that had burst in, sweaty and panting. Ha, he could use a shower himself.

The '*Poirot*' lookalike got out on the floor below Jake's, leaving her with a barely disguised "Hurumph." Kat rolled her eyes and shook her head.

Of course, Jake didn't answer the door so Kat let herself in again, calling round the door to avoid any surprises. No answer, so she made her way inside.

"Jake? You ready yet, it's," the security monitor on the wall in the hallway was showing the time in big, bold numbers, "Seven thirty." Yes! She'd made it bang on time.

The living room was empty, his work desk by the window clean and neat, the beginnings of a new *Princess Sparkles* episode starting to take shape, in crude pencil lines.

"Jake! Come on, it's time." Not in the kitchen. The worktops were spotless, even the dishes from the night before washed and put away. She had to admit she was a little impressed.

The bedroom door was closed, so she rapped loudly and called again. "Seriously, Jake, it's time to go. I'm coming in and if you're sleeping there's going to be trouble." This wasn't like him at all, he was always punctual.

She peered through the door. She'd not seen the inside of his bedroom before. It was a good size, the clean, bright white décor continued through into here. The vast king-sized bed was made (of course) and she could hear the fan running in the en-suite. So that's where he is. She pounded on the door, "Jake, come on, we're going to be late!"

No answer. Okay, this was worrying. "Jake," she resumed in a worried tone, "are you okay in there? Look, I'm going to come in."

She opened the door a crack – no sounds of protest, so she opened it all the way and stepped in. Jeez, this was nearly as big as her living room. But it was empty. Stepping over a discarded towel by the sink, she checked the shower, also empty – but there was still a little steam in the air, so he MUST have used the shower not very long ago.

Now, she was really starting to get worried. She hurried out, into the living room, peered through the large folding glass doors onto the terrace garden. Not there, she tried the door – locked.

The guest bathroom was empty. That other door turned out to be a large store room – or it could have been a box room. But no Jake, no sign of him at all.

Surely, he hadn't gone out, that would be the last

thing he'd do. She tried calling his mobile... a low buzzing sound from the bedroom made her heart sink. She followed the sound and found his phone by the bed. She hung up. The apartment was silent, apart from the thrum of the extractor.

Kat leaned inside the bathroom to turn off the light. There was no pull-cord, but outside there was a switch on the wall by the door. The light turned off, but the fan continued running on a timer.

Lost for what to do, she looked around the bedroom for any kind of clue.

Neatly laid out on the bed were what she assumed were the clothes he'd planned to wear today. So that ruled out the unlikely scenario that he'd just upped and gone off without her... Then she saw it.

Was he taking the piss? That t-shirt. Was he really going to turn up to a comic signing wearing a *Princess Sparkles* shirt? She'd thought it was just an ordinary white shirt, but the neatly machine-embroidered little 'P.S.' with sequin rainbow was unmistakable.

She sat down heavily on the bed and dialled Jerome. Maybe they'd spoken?

"Jerome, hi it's Kat."

"Kat, hi can you be quick?" Came the flustered response, "I'm at the main hall and the bloody handouts haven't arrived yet." In the background she could hear banging and yelling of the exhibition crew shifting boxes and equipment about.

"Have you spoken with Jake? Like, today or last night?"

"Jake? No, aren't you both supposed to be on the way here by now?" His voice had gone up a semitone.

"No, I'm at his apartment and he's not here! He can't have gone out, you know what he's like."

"For the love of– okay, okay, look can I leave this with you, It's all going to crap here. We should have been set last night and we've not even got the signoff on the stand build from the safety inspector."

"Sure, leave it with me, I'll get back if I find him." She hung up. Jerome had tried to save money this year and had his own contractors put together the exhibition stand but of course only UNION workers were allowed to work at the illustrious Earl's Court exhibition centre and the red tape had caught up with him. She'd *told* him that would happen.

The fan suddenly shut off in the bathroom. The silence was eerie.

So, that was it then. All she could do was stay here at Jake's apartment until he showed up. If he'd gone out then he'd certainly be back soon, and likely in a bad way.

She remembered that he'd tried it last summer, braving the warm evening to go get a– there was a sound. What was that? Some kind of squeak. No way he had rodents in the apartment!

She stood and listened carefully. Nothing. No, there it was again, a muffled squeak. Where was it coming from? Again, there, the bathroom. She hurried over, turned on the light and poked her head through the door.

Nothing. Then she saw a small movement on the floor, the towel. There was something in there, and it made a sound again.

Cautiously, she bent down to see.

"What the–" a small, fat, pink nose pushed its way out from the crumpled towel. It wriggled a little, and then a tiny paw stretched out from underneath. If the morning wasn't strange enough, there was a tiny puppy wrapped up in a towel on Jake's bathroom floor.

Since when did Jake have a puppy? She picked it up, just a couple of handfuls of tan coloured fur. It can't be more than a month old.

He would have told her about it yesterday, or she would have seen it or heard it. What's more he wouldn't have just *bought* a puppy, he'd have got all the paraphernalia that went with it – bed, feeding bowls, toys, bags of food. There was none of that around that she could see, though knowing Jake, most of it would have been neatly put away.

And why leave it alone in the bathroom? Too many questions here, and none of it added up.

"Unless…" she said out loud. The pup opened its eyes, yawned and then closed them again. "This isn't Jake's puppy. That makes sense. Who's puppy are you?"

That DID kind of make sense. Perhaps someone – let's worry about who later – had just dropped a puppy off in an emergency and left in a hurry. The bathroom WOULD be a good place to leave it for a short while – easier to clean up. There! Mystery solved. Jake must have gone out to get supplies. That must have taken all his courage. Her mind was whirling now as she tried to put all the pieces together.

She brought the puppy with her into the bedroom and laid it on the towel on the bed, shifted the clothes onto a chair and sat cross-legged on the bed watching it.

It... she picked it up... ah, it was a HE. On his cute, fat pink tummy, he had a brown birthmark just above his little– "UGH! PFFT! No, no, you monster!" Of course, you should never, *ever* hold a puppy up to your face like that. 100% guaranteed it'll PEE on you!

Kat plopped the puppy down on the towel and ran to the bathroom, stripping off her shirt and throwing it onto the floor. She quickly splashed water onto her face, front and hair. Patting herself dry with a towel from the pile behind her, sniffing to make sure she'd got it all off.

"This really isn't how I'd expected to be spending my morning." She lamented, then went on the hunt for a t-shirt she could borrow.

Jake's wardrobe and drawers were almost sickeningly neat, everything folded and hung up in order. So, happily she was able to find a cool, black *Rising Flesh* t-shirt with a red skull on it.

She returned to the bed and lay facing the puppy.

"So, where's Jake?" she asked softly. "The pet store won't be open for ages yet. The only place open would be the 24/7 just along the road." Probably doable with Jake's condition – if he HAD to. But he'd be back by now.

She sat up, cross-legged on the bed, sighed. If she was in it for the day then she needed coffee. She'd missed out this morning but at least she'd have time for one now.

Checking that the puppy was still curled up in the towel, she made her way to the kitchen in search of caffeinated salvation.

It wasn't hard to find everything. He only had two,

plain white mugs, everything else was pared down to the absolute essentials, the cutlery only seemed to have six of everything because they usually came like that in a set.

No instant coffee, but there was a packet of expensive looking ground stuff in a bag in the fridge.

That would do nicely, thanks Jake. It took a couple of minutes to figure out why he didn't have a kettle. The sink had one of those crazy instant hot water taps that also produced chilled and... get this, SPARKLING water.

She texted Jerome while the coffee brewed. He'd be running about like a headless chicken right now, she guessed, and a phone call might send him over the edge.

[KAT] Jake still missing. Box of signed editions of series 8 under my desk - figured might come in handy one day. Maybe can sell to pntrs instd. Get Mario to bring them up to Lndn.

A few minutes later, she was back on the bed, cradling some pretty amazing coffee and wondering what to do next. It was too soon to call the police, and to be fair he probably wasn't in any real danger.

At that moment, her phone chimed and the puppy woke. It was Jerome

[JEROME B] Genius idea! Thx.

Sometimes she felt like she was babysitting Jake and Jerome. Jerome should be better organised but she didn't really mind helping Jake out.

The puppy had started crawling about, mewling plaintively. It looked hungry. Who knew when it had last eaten. She should get it something.

Kat picked up the wriggling little bundle and took it to the kitchen. She remembered that the milk in Jake's fridge was the filtered, organic, extra cream variety.

Slightly warmed up in the microwave, the little pup lapped it up greedily then sat in the bowl with a happy expression on its face, burped and curled up to sleep.

"Well, that was easy. But I think we need to get you something proper to eat." The time on her phone showed 8:19. She sat on the tiles for a couple of minutes and watched the puppy sleep.

"Let's give it until lunchtime. He won't eat out, so he'll HAVE to be back by then."

The puppy grumbled a little in its sleep as Kat picked it up and fetched the towel from the bedroom. She made a little nest for it on the couch and picked up the TV remote from the basket under the coffee table.

Jake hadn't skimped on the TV, it was enormous and started up with a soothing chime. To her delight, Kat found that the smart TV had plenty of streaming apps loaded. This wasn't going to be so bad.

She paused her third episode of *The Walking Dead*, suddenly realising that she'd spent the whole morning binging the new series. It was past 1pm, her stomach was complaining and the puppy was up and about, exploring the makeshift nest and chewing experimentally at a corner of the towel.

"Ah, no you don't." She picked it up and prised the soggy corner from needle-sharp teeth. "I think we both need lunch." There was a great noodle bar very close that did really good ramen. That was another good thing about living over in this part of town, everything was right on your doorstep.

"Okay, let's put you away safely while I get us some lunch. Jake's going to owe me for this." She leant over to pick up the towel – it wasn't pretty! "Oh, crap – Jake's towel." It was a goner. Happily, the mess hadn't soaked through onto the couch or she'd be toast.

The soiled towel went into the shower to be dealt with later and another, clean one was offered up for sacrifice as a bed in the bathroom.

"Be good. Won't be long." She blew a little kiss, carefully closed the door and headed out.

About an hour later, Kat struggled through the door, laden with what she hoped would be what was needed to take care of the puppy. She was half hoping that Jake would be back by now; two tubs of spicy beef ramen dangled in a carrier bag from a couple of sore fingers.

Clearly, Jake was still out in the wilderness. She dumped her supplies in the middle of the living room and let the puppy out of the bathroom. It was awake and wobbled out happily, sniffing the air hungrily.

Another towel was trashed, and the floor was horrendous. That would have to wait until after lunch – she closed the door but left the fan on. The little puppy scampered hopefully after her to the kitchen.

The assistant in the pet store had been brilliant. Kat had guessed that it was about a month old and was sold a supply of puppy milk, solid food and plenty of absorbent mats, cleaning sprays and a huge industrial sized roll of blue paper towel – *that's going to come in handy for the bathroom*, she thought.

Pup had greedily scoffed down a packet of meat and was curled up on a mat in the living room by the time Kat was half way through her noodles. The TV was on again. Just ONE more episode before the big clean up...

Kat looked dubiously at the bin-liner full of paper towels as she sipped a coffee. The bathroom had survived, but those two towels... no chance. Jake's fault for being so reckless. She'd left the receipt for the puppy supplies out on his desk too. He could pay for all that.

Enough. Half past five, and no show. Outside, the sky had turned a deep dusky mauve. Kat sat up straight, cleared her throat. There was no *actual* emergency so she dialled 111 rather than 999. Within a few seconds, she was through to a local police station.

"Hi Um, I'd like to report a missing person please. I know I should wait 24 hours before calling, but I'm really worried." she gabbled nervously.

The police officer on duty explained that this wasn't the case, it was fine to call as soon as someone went missing especially if they were vulnerable. He calmly took details, his full name, his address and description, though of course she couldn't say what he was wearing. She'd need to head back home for her laptop to email them a recent photo of him which she happened to have.

"Okay ma'am that should do for now. Please, try not to worry. We'll check the local A&E and patrols will be on the lookout for him." The officer had a deep, reassuring tone "Keep your phone switched on and we'll call back as soon as we have anything."

That was a relief. Kat felt that she ought to have called earlier, then the police might have picked him up by now. She felt a pang of guilt.

Puppy was awake and had been watching her on the phone with his head cocked slightly to one side.

"Oh, pup, you're just so cute." She picked him up and cuddled him "I've got to go out for a little while, so it's back in the bathroom again for you." He laid his head against her arm and looked at her with his lovely brown eyes.

Kat could feel her heart melting. She wiped her eyes and set him down on the floor. "I'll leave you with a bit of dinner."

About half an hour later Kat returned with a duffel bag over her shoulder, dumped it on the sofa and headed towards the bedroom.

"Hey Pup," she whispered, "I'm back. Did you eat up all your–" She stopped dead. The bathroom door was wide open, the light from the door spilling into the darkness of the bedroom.

"Shit," she breathed, "I'm sure I closed it." The puppy had got out of the bathroom. Fortunately, the bedroom door was closed, so he'd be somewhere in here.

A ragged gasp behind her in the dark froze her in her tracks. In the gloom, a large mass was slowly moving on the bed. As it shifted, the light from the bathroom caught a pair of eyes – human eyes.

"Jake! Oh my God!" She sprinted to the bed and

threw her arms around his neck. Then she jumped back, startled. "Jake, you're naked; and *so* cold."

Jake groaned, delirious; his ashen face turned towards her, pain, anguish.

"You're sick." she whispered, folding the duvet over his curled form. She tucked it all around him so that all that showed was his tortured visage. "What happened? Where did you go?" she pleaded.

"I..." The effort to speak was almost too much, his eyelids fluttered then his vision focused on her face, half-lit, "I can't remember. Just you, calling. Just now. Blackness."

"I've got to call an ambulance. Oh, crap do you think you've got COVID?"

"I don't know." He seemed to be coming to his senses a little "I don't think so... give me a moment." He closed his eyes as if in thought, breathing slowly and regularly.

"Do you want me to get you a hot drink? You're freezing." Kat asked, then remembered "Where's the puppy?"

He opened his eyes and cocked his head quizzically, "What puppy?"

CHAPTER 3

"WHAT DO YOU mean 'what puppy', the one I've been looking after all day while you were... I dunno, *walking the earth* like one of your *Rising Flesh.*"

A little colour was starting to come back into Jake's face. He wriggled about a bit, the folded duvet was making him feel like a taco "Seriously, I don't have any idea what you're talking about."

"Don't you remember *anything* from today? Are you sure you didn't accidentally let it out when you came in?" Kat was pacing now, looking under the bed, behind the curtains.

"No, nothing. All I remember is waking up here, in bed. Freezing and just... well, so tired."

"I'm going to check the hallway." Came Kat's voice from the bathroom. The shower door slid open and closed. A few seconds later, the toilet seat clanked.

"Don't go anywhere." Kat's voice, suddenly loud in Jakes's face startled him from a light doze.

Outside in the hallway, all was quiet; no sign of the mysterious puppy. It was just a single carpeted passage, all the way down to the lift. The little lobby area had a couple of high-backed chairs there and a table with a vase and a lamp that she'd never even really looked at in nearly two years of coming here. Kat checked under and behind them both, stopped to listen to the lift glide quietly between floors down below then made her way back to the apartment.

While she was gone, Jake had flipped the duvet so that he was properly underneath it to get a bit more comfortable – and protect his modesty.

"I'm going to leave a note on the pin board down in the main lobby, maybe someone's seen him," she announced, "and go put on some clothes while I'm gone if you're feeling shy. Don't worry," she quipped over her shoulder "I've seen it all before!" Jake pulled the duvet tighter under his chin and shivered.

After the door had clicked shut, Jake swung his legs over the side of the bed and sat for a moment. Every muscle in his body felt like it had cramped. He took a breath and pulled himself unsteadily to his feet.

Four pairs of identical dark blue shorts and charcoal grey t-shirts lay neatly folded in a wardrobe drawer. He pulled them on like an old man, and flopped back down onto the bed, pulling the duvet back up around himself against the chill. He had never felt so frightened in his life. Somehow a whole day had just been ripped away from him. He was used to order, neatness and control in his life. It filled the void that was left behind after– he took a long, ragged breath... after his parents had died.

"Knock, Knock. It's me, are you decent?" Kat called softly through the bedroom door.

"Yeah," he answered weakly, "come in."

Kat sat on the edge of the bed and placed her palm on his forehead. Not quite so cold now. To Jake, the warmth of her hand was like sunshine, and he ventured a smile.

"I think you're on the mend. Do you want to eat? I got you some ramen this afternoon while you were out and I've still got some left. I can heat it up if you like?"

"Sure." He tried to think of the last time someone had made him hot food when he was sick, "I could definitely eat."

"Right. I'll bung it in the microwave, come on out in a couple of minutes."

Kat had found a couple of large bowls to transfer the noodles into and was giving the first heated one a stir when Jake shuffled into the kitchen. He had the duvet over his shoulders looking for all the world like the ghostly figures you might see 'early' in the morning at a music festival, tired, hung over hunting down bacon sandwiches and coffee.

The microwave hummed in the background, timer counting down while the rich aroma filled the kitchen. "Here, I didn't make it too hot. Hope you like Spicy beef."

"Smells good. Thanks."

"You want to eat it in here or the living room?" she asked, popping the oven open as it beeped.

"Coffee table's fine. I'll get some chopsticks and spoons." He drifted to the counter and pulled out the utensils.

"Um. Just a fork for me thanks. Never got the hang of chopsticks. I've got a spoon here already." She waved it and licked the sauce from it, grinning sheepishly.

"I'll have to teach you some day." He replied halfway out the door.

"Yes." Kat said softly, half to herself, "Yes, that would be nice."

Jake was already tucking into his noodles and soup when Kat joined him with the remains of her lunch from earlier. She sat on the couch and started slowly twirling her fork to pick up noodles.

"You eat your noodles like spaghetti." He smiled, slurping the thin yellow strands from his chopsticks "This is the *only* way."

"I think I'd starve before I learned how to do that." She chuckled. "Jake, you seriously can't remember where you got that puppy from?"

"No. Like I said, the whole day's just been a total blank. He gulped down some of the rich, spicy soup with a ceramic Chinese soup spoon. "I really hope it's okay. If I'd have let it out by accident, it couldn't have gone far."

"Yeah, most likely with a neighbour. I didn't fancy knocking on any doors just now. Perhaps I will in the morning if we don't hear anything."

"Kat," He turned to look at her, he often avoided eye contact, but this time his large, brown eyes locked onto hers, tearing a little, "Kat, I really appreciate your help today. I don't know what would have happened if you hadn't been there for me."

"That's okay Jake, I'm just happy that you're okay now."

They sat in silence eating their meal, punctuated by slurps and the clinks of cutlery.

Afterwards, they got into a deep conversation about the plotline for Jake's zombie comic series. Kat was still confused as to why Jake had suddenly killed off the central character, but he reassured her that he knew what he was doing.

Kat picked up her phone to see if there were any messages from Jerome. She'd totally forgotten about him. None. Well, no news is good news as they say. She noticed the time was a little before eleven. Not her usual time to sleep but she was surprised that the time had passed so quickly. She yawned, it had been a hell of a day.

"Jake, I'm still worried about you. Do you think I should crash here tonight, just in case?"

"I think I feel better, but this whole thing has really shaken me." He admitted, "I normally wouldn't ask, but I think I'd feel better having you about. If you want to take the bed, I'll rough it on the couch here, I've got a blanket I can use."

"Nah, I reckon if we stick some pillows in between, we could make that massive bed of yours work for the both of us... If you promise no monkey business!" She laughed and elbowed him.

"I don't think you need to worry about that," he replied, rubbing his side, "that's the last thing on my mind right now."

"Okay, then," she chirped, "we'd be like Bert and Ernie."

"More like Morecombe and wise." Jake suggested, and they both laughed.

"You know," Kat said heading into the bathroom with her duffel bag, "I only brought this over because I was worried you *weren't* going to come back any time soon."

"I believe you." Jake called back as the door closed. He waited, sat up in bed for Kat to shower and get changed. He shuffled the row of pillows on his right side and patted them down. He'd go see his doctor on Monday, they ought to give him an emergency appointment because of his present list of mental health issues. Hopefully, this was just a blip and he'd be fine.

Kat emerged from the bathroom wearing a pair of cosy looking plaid pyjamas. She'd untied her ponytail and her slightly damp blonde hair hung about her shoulders. "That's one powerful shower! I'm sure it even exfoliates!" she joked, sitting on the bed next to Jake towelling off her hair. "I found your razor on the floor under the sink just now, I put it under the mirror for you."

"Wait, I remember that. I was going to shave, just got out of the shower... Terrible headache, heart racing... Then..."

"Then what? Keep going it's starting to come back."

"No. That's all. Nothing until I woke up."

"But the bathroom door was open, so you MUST have seen it when you came back. Remembered that you found a puppy somewhere?"

"Found. Maybe I bought it from someone."

"No, I'm sure you didn't buy it. Where would you have kept your wallet?" she laughed. "But that's kind of good news."

"Good news? How?"

"Well, at least you LEFT the apartment naked. You didn't go out in a haze and then GET naked somewhere."

"That's not much comfort."

"No," she admitted, "I guess not." She reached into

her bag and pulled out a book, "Do you mind if I read for a while? You sleep if you need to."

"No, that's fine. I'm just so tired. Thanks again Kat."

"Night, Jake," She made a kissing sound, Jake smiled, turned around and settled down to sleep.

Kat sat up in bed for a few minutes, going over the day in her head. Somehow, she felt at ease, maybe it was just because this whole crazy day had come to an end; Jake was safe, hopefully a neighbour would turn in the puppy.

She picked up her book from the bedside table and read a few pages, but she kept going over the same line, her head nodding. Don't fight it, you're beat, girl. With that, she put the book back, turned off the light and was asleep in a matter of minutes.

CHAPTER 4

Sunday 14-March 2021.

Moonrise: 07:08. Set 19:12. 1.4%
Sunset: 18:08.

KAT WOKE SLOWLY, eyes still closed. God, this was a comfortable bed. That's what money brings, I guess.

Suddenly, she was aware of warm breath in her ear, a closeness, a soft tongue against her earlobe. She giggled at the tickling.

"Jake, remember we agreed." She turned to face him, all smiles, "No monkey business." Then her eyes focused. "PUPPY! Oh my God, you're home! Oh, Jake, you got him back, oh you're amazing." She threw her arms around the happy little bundle who now got down to the serious business of face licking and tail wagging. She got up on one elbow to peer over the pillows, "Jake, where was...." Oh, not there. She'd been talking to herself. She sat up and looked again at the puppy. Was she imagining it or was he a lot bigger than she remembered him? You know what, yes this can't be the same one. "Are you an imposter?" she whispered. He cocked his head to one side, then threw himself into her lap, legs in the air demanding belly rubs – ah, okay yes, "Ha! Clever boy. Identity confirmed." The distinctive birthmark was there for all to see... Amongst other things.

"Come on Pup, let's see if your daddy's made you breakfast yet." She threw off the duvet and the little dog jumped to the floor. Jake's nightclothes were scrunched up in the bed.

"Hey, Jake. Good job getting the–" She went cold. The puppy scampering behind pulled on the brakes and skidded into the back of her legs. The kitchen was empty, as was the living room which she'd just passed through.

"No." Her voice breaking, "No, no, no not again." Tears started to roll down her face, tears of frustration.

"Fuck, Jake. I can't do this again. Where ARE you!" she screamed, sinking to the tiled floor in uncontrollable sobs. The puppy approached her slowly, nudging under her elbow and whimpering.

"Oh, puppy it's not your fault. I'm not angry with you," She sniffed, and he laid his head in her lap looking up at her, "I'm just scared for Jake. He's sick and he's lost and alone."

The door intercom chimed. The puppy raised his head, floppy yellow ears alert.

"Do you think it's him? Is he back?" she said, hoping, wanting it to be so. The screen showed two police officers at the outer door. The smaller, female officer looked up into the camera. Ice ran through Kat's veins. What could this mean? Oh, please no. She buzzed the officers up and stood, in front of the door waiting for them to arrive, biting her thumb nail.

The doorbell chimed, and Kat opened the door to the police officers.

"Katherine Benson, is it?" the male officer asked.

Kat nodded , still biting her nail. The puppy sat at her feet, leaning against her leg, tail wagging uncertainly.

"Nothing to worry about Miss Benson. I'm PC Colin

Rust and this is my colleague WPC Alice Poole. We're following up from your missing person report last night. Has the gentleman returned at all?"

"Um. Yes, and well, no. Please, come in." Kat ushered the two inside into the living room.

WPC Poole knelt down and tickled the puppy behind the ear, "He's a little sweetie isn't he?" The puppy wagged his tail and licked at the officer's hand. "What's his name?"

This stumped Kat for a moment, and she had to force back tears again, then everything just poured out "I don't... Sorry, I don't know, he's Jake's dog. He got him before he went missing, then he was back and now he's gone and I don't know what's going on and I... I..." Poole led her, sobbing to the couch and sat next to her for a moment while she composed herself. Rust hung back to let his partner deal with this part.

"Katherine, it's okay. We're here to help, just take a moment if you need to and we can go through some more details at your own pace. Now, the good news is that we haven't had any reports of anybody matching Jake's description at the hospitals, or on CCTV. That's very encouraging, though I have to say it's a little puzzling because the area outside the building is well covered."

Kat, wiped her eyes with the sleeves of her pyjamas and took a slow breath.

"So, tell me." Poole continued, "What happened yesterday when he came back?"

Kat relayed the events of the last 24 hours as best as she could remember, while Officer Rust took notes in a little black spiral bound notepad. Satisfied that she'd got all the information that Kat was likely to be able to provide, Poole stood and looked over to Rust, who nodded.

"Okay then Katherine, I think that's all for now. We're going to continue to do our best to find Jake, and we'll be able to help refer him to someone who can help him afterwards."

"Oh, sorry I didn't say," Kat sniffed, getting to her feet, "Jake has a guy that he talks with every so often about his mental health issues, he does it online mostly so I'll ask him to make an appointment."

"That's good," Rust hadn't spoken at all while Kat was giving her statement, his voice was deep and rich, and she thought she recognised his soft Yorkshire accent from the phone call last night, but she couldn't remember who she spoke with, "there's a lot of folk that don't take good care of their mental health. It's a good sign that he's got a handle on things."

Kat nodded, without speaking.

"There's one more line of enquiry that we could try," he began, "it's a long shot but it might give some clues as to Jake's movements."

Kat brightened a little, this was new "Sure, anything, what can I do?"

Rust took a black rucksack with police markings from his back, Kat hadn't seen this at all until now.

"I also do some work with the police canine unit, and help with dog and other pet incidents." He brought a device out of the bag, it was no larger than his outstretched hand and looked a little like a car steering wheel. "It looks like this little chap is about six months old, am I right?"

Kat did a mental double-take, "N– uh, y– yes, I suppose." she stammered. The policeman was right, he *did* look about six months old.

"Good. So, all being well by this age he'll be microchipped. It's the law, and we'll be able to look up information about where this was done, and maybe trace the original owners or breeders."

Kat nodded; that was a really good idea. PC Rust knelt next to the puppy. The scanner beeped once as he switched it on. He placed it against the back of pup's neck for a second or two. Nothing, he tried a couple more times, and looked up to Kat, frowning.

"No. Sorry, looks like your little chap here's not chipped. A professional breeder would have had him chipped by eight weeks."

"So, Jake must have got him from, like a private sale or something?"

"Probably, yes, but there *is* still a legal responsibility to chip a dog. If you like, I can help you with that. Part of what I do is to help people in the community to get their dogs chipped and registered. It can be a great help if, God forbid, you ever lose him."

Kat shuddered at the thought. "You're right, yes. Does it hurt?"

Rust shook his head, "No, it's just a little pinch. Most dogs hardly notice it. I often carry my kit with me, so I can do it now if you like. It's a new thing we're trying, on the spot. There's no fee, and it saves all the hassle of prosecuting anyone who fails to get it done."

Kat agreed and filled in a short online form on her phone with Jake's details as the owner.

Rust produced a slightly intimidating tool, like a

chunky syringe and loaded a rice-grain sized capsule into it.

"Just hold on to him for a moment, talk to him to distract him so he won't wriggle." Rust instructed.

It was over in a moment, the little dog made a little yelp and a sneezing sound, then jumped up to lick Kat's face.

Poole stifled a little giggle "Did you hear that? It sounded like he swore."

Kat giggled from underneath a fury of yellow fluffy exuberance. "Yes, I think he did," then to the puppy, "Didntchoo, clever boy!" She was feeling a little better now. Some of the metallic-edged fear had gone from her stomach.

"I think it's safe to assume that he's not vaccinated either." Suggested Rust, zipping up the scanner into a tidy black pouch. "There's a decent vet attached to the big pet store on Hartley Road."

"Yeah, I know the place." Kat put in.

"You might get a drop-in appointment if you go down there during the week." Came Rust's advice.

"So, I think that just about wraps things up for now." Poole began, "We're going to keep on the look out, and we'll stay in touch. Do you have any questions at all?"

Kat shook her head and gave the puppy a little hug. She got up to take a card from Poole. "You can get in touch with me directly on this number if you need to."

With that, the two officers left.

"Okay, fellah." she said. "Just us for a while. Let's get you some breakfast." The puppy yapped happily and followed Kat into the kitchen.

By mid-afternoon, most of Kat's enthusiasm had evaporated again. She had a couple of weepy moments worrying about Jake as the sun headed towards the west, behind the taller buildings in town. There were still a couple of hours of daylight left, and as the sun sank, the anxiety built, hoping that he'd return again before dark.

"I can't stay inside any longer!" she cried, "we need to get out for a while." She looked at the puppy, it was chewing industriously on a plush dinosaur she'd got him yesterday. He stopped, looked up and gave his tail an uncertain wag.

"Okay, come on, let's take a walk round the park, get some air." Kat grabbed a piece of paper and scribbled a note on it on the off-chance that Jake returned when she was out – sod's law of course that he would.

Kat grabbed her warm fleece, phone, lead, doggy bags... Oh, lead. She rummaged about in the big carrier bag of dog stuff and pulled out a cute blue lead and collar with dinosaurs woven into it (she'd kind of gone for a theme there).

"You *have* grown." she mumbled, extending the collar to nearly the maximum adjustment. It was the clip-type which turned out to be a good choice as the puppy excitedly wriggled about. He yapped and scratched at the new collar for a moment until Kat dangled the lead at him. That got his attention, and he tried to grab at it.

There was nobody about in the quiet apartment block as they took the lift down and into the lobby. The note had gone from the pin-board, hopefully Jake had taken it down rather than some busybody.

The outer door clicked automatically to unlock as they approached it but the puppy sat resolutely at the threshold, face pointed down to the ground as if it couldn't bear to look at the pavement outside.

"Come on you, we're going to the park – all dogs love the park!" she enthused. Nope. Not moving. Kat tried pulling on the lead, but he just lay flat on the tiles, legs splayed.

"Seriously. Come on, let's go!" she coaxed, but the puppy was having none of it. Kat knelt down and saw that he was shivering. "You're really scared aren't you?" He looked up into her eyes and whimpered, big brown eyes pleading.

"Okay," she said softly, scratching behind his ear, "we'll spend the evening in. Just you and me..." Then she realised what she'd said and a lump formed in her throat, "come on then." she croaked, voice breaking.

The sun had set about an hour ago and Kat was curled up on the sofa under a big blanket that she'd found, puppy was snuggled up next to her. The TV, ignored ran on though some Netflix Manga series that she hoped would distract her. If Jake had any schedule to his disappearances, he was late by now.

Puppy jerked in his sleep, his paws twitching in a running rhythm, he made a couple of muffled yelps. Kat turned her bloodshot eyes to watch his nocturnal adventures unfold.

Suddenly, he sat bolt upright. Kat's eyes darted towards the hallway into the shadows towards the door. Was there a sound there? Both sat rigid, listening for several seconds, then the little dog shook it's head, yelped, scratched at its ear.

"You got a flea there?" Kat asked, amused. But the pup yelped again, shook it's head and growled. It stopped for a moment, then howled in pain.

Kat jumped up. Something was very wrong. "Oh, puppy, what's the matter?" she leant in to try to comfort him when he yelped and a cloud of dust hit her in the face, where it came from she couldn't see. The shock knocked her back onto her bottom and she came to rest on the floor between the sofa and the coffee table.

There was a kind of mist forming around the puppy, golden brown, swirling gently as if it were alive.

At once, the puppy yelped and the cloud of mist convulsed and collapsed towards the agonised form. More mist appeared from the air around, forming filaments and clumps, slowly drifting inwards like smoke filmed in reverse.

The edges of the puppy were beginning to blur now and it seemed to be gaining volume as the cloud slowly sucked inwards. A cough rang out, choking as the puppy clawed at the blue collar around its neck, twisting his head back and forth to try to get a purchase on it with its teeth, but it was futile. The puppy continued to gain mass and choke.

Suddenly, Kat came to her senses – he was strangling, the collar was too tight. She threw herself forward and reached for the collar through the golden cloud. It pulled at her skin, it was warm but left her feeling icy to the bones inside. Her fingers fumbled for the clip, but the collar was starting to become buried in a strange mush that was beginning to form – almost a liquid, but it wasn't clinging to her fingers. It pulled back like rubber towards the puppy's neck as she scrabbled. All the time, the Puppy's breathing became worse, ragged, desperate.

At last she found the clip and pressed the two sides together and felt it release. The collar pushed out from the puppy's neck by the living liquid flesh and fell loose in her hands.

Kat jumped back as the puppy took a huge breath. It had stopped yelping now and sat upright, hardly moving, allowing the cloud to envelop it in accelerating swathes, blurring his form until he was barely visible.

And suddenly, it stopped. The last of the mist slammed into the body, laying inert on the couch and was gone.

The inert body... of a man, lay curled in a ball on the sofa, back glistening with sweat.

A ragged gasp of breath broke the silence, and Jake coughed, long and hard.

The collar dropped from Kat's hand with a clatter. Her hand was shaking, face ashen, eyes wild with terror utterly unable to comprehend what she had just witnessed.

CHAPTER 5

JAKE STIRRED, GROANED and curled himself a little tighter on the couch. Behind him, Kat was beginning to hyperventilate, fists balled at her sides, chest heaving in silent screams. Soon, hoarse rasps came, until she was able to finally scream and scream.

As the first scream rang out Jake jerked alert and tumbled untidily to the floor at Kat's feet, he held his palms against the sides of his head against the noise, eyes screwed tight.

She managed about six full-throated yells before she was able to begin to compose herself and stood panting, gasping, reaching deep within her body and her mind for words.

The fire in her brain and the rushing sound in her ears subsided and she fell to her knees burying her face in the back of Jake's neck, sobbing.

"Jake... you, it was... It was you." She managed. Jake turned his head and rolled over a little to face her.

"I was choking." he whispered, putting a hand to his neck and rubbing it, "You saved me."

"But how were you the puppy?" A tear dropped onto Jake's chest, "I don't understand, what happened."

"I don't either," Jake croaked, "I think I remember some things. I remember you were there, and I was scared... Something scared me. The street, I think."

"Yes. Yes, that's right, I tried to take the pu– I tried to take you out for a little walk." She sat down on the floor, cross-legged starting to come to her senses.

"You were too scared to go out. You can't go out, so yes, nor could the puppy, I mean you as a puppy."

A sudden rap on the door made her start, and she jumped to her feet. Who could be at the door at this time?

Kat peered through the spy-hole, it was *Poirot* from the lift the other day. What could he want? She opened the door a little.

"Will you filthy animals keep it down!" he raged through gritted teeth "My poor Foufou is traumatised."

Kat was caught off-guard, "Foufou?" was about all she could come up with.

"Foufou, *girl*," his neat little moustache twitched, "is my little Chihuahua."

That was too much for Kat. She stifled a laugh, snorted and tried to keep the remainder back by clamping a hand to her mouth.

"I think you've got it wrong." She squeaked through her fingers, "I saw a big spider." Her shoulders heaved up and down. *Poirot's* eyes darted over Kat's shoulders, widened in disbelief as Jake stumbled past towards the bedroom, naked and beginning to retch.

"That, madam," he snorted, "is no spider." And with that he turned on his heels and left.

Kat quickly slammed the door and slid down against it to the floor breathless with laughter. After a minute, she felt that was really what she needed to release the tension. She cleared her throat and went to see how Jake was faring.

"What was that all about?" Jake asked, sipping from a large glass of water. He'd put on his standard issue shorts and t-shirt and was sitting on the bed.

"Honestly, you don't want to know." Kat chuckled, sitting beside him, "It was weird. But I think right now you win the golden prize for weird."

Jake nodded, "Yeah, this is really some messed up shit."

Kat put a hand to his forehead, "How are you feeling?"

He paused, taking stock, "Not too bad. I feel like I've been put through a meat grinder still but not so bad as yesterday. That was awful."

"You know, in a way a part of me feels a little relieved." Kat rationalised, "At least you were here, safe. I looked after you all weekend, I fed you... you... you peed in my face!" They looked at each other, and the ridiculousness of the situation hit him first. He snorted, then collapsed into a kind of exhausted spasm of laughter.

"I'm a *werewolf*, for God's sake!"

"No," she was laughing so hard now that she wanted to pee "No, you're a were*PUPPY*!" Kat laughed.

"How's that even possible? That's all just made-up stuff in movies and comic books. There's not even a full moon!"

"Perhaps it doesn't work like that? Maybe you're only a puppy..." she stifled a giggle, "sorry, only a puppy in the day?"

"I don't know if that's true." He had composed himself now, he wanted to understand what was happening to him; but where to start? "It's night time now, the sun went down hours ago."

"So, it's something else that triggers it. You were

having a dream, running or something when you turned back, could it be an emotional thing?"

"Like the incredible hulk? He goes all green when he's angry. Not much of a super-power being a puppy. What kind of a puppy anyhow?"

"Hmmm, I'm not really sure. NOT a wolf though – maybe a Labrador? Golden Retriever? Floppy ears and cute, fat little tummy."

"I had no idea." He shook his head, tears welling in his eyes now, "What's happening to me?"

She scooted over on the bed and held him tightly, "I really don't know, but let's get through this together. I could take a couple of days off work. It started all by itself, maybe it'll just go away by itself? Besides, you could do with a dog-sitter!"

"Okay," He turned and smiled at her, "that would be really helpful."

"I'm going to need to go get a few more things if I'm staying a couple more days." Kat decided. "Will you be okay while I'm gone?"

Jake sniffed and rubbed his eyes, "Yeah, I'm starting to feel okay now. Why don't you just leave your washing here, I'll bung it in the washer. I'll cook us up something to eat as well? I'm famished. Should be ready by the time you're back, I guess."

It took Kat two bumps to open her door this time. After just a couple of days away, the smell of damp was very noticeable. A small pile of letters were waiting for her on the floor which she scooped up and thrust into her empty bag.

The spilled milk from several days ago in the kitchen

made its presence abundantly clear. She cleaned it up and disposed of the manky dishcloth and the few remaining elderly items from the fridge in a white bin bag.

Finally, a selection of clothes, her laptop plus charger and essential toiletries were shoved into the bulging bag.

The leather portfolio from Friday was still on the end of the couch – *shit*, she thought. *I'm going to need to be in work tomorrow.*

Kat took a last look around the dingy room, grabbed the artwork and left.

Dinner was ready when Kat got back, and her clothes merrily tumbling in the washer. She offered to clean up the kitchen after they ate, but Jake had left the kitchen spotless, cleaning as he cooked.

Kat placed her fork onto her plate with deliberate care, "Jake, that was delicious. Thanks so much – where did you learn to cook like that?"

"The internet, mostly," he laughed "there's a *lot* of cookery videos out there. That and a lot of practice."

Kat took the plates to the kitchen and washed them, feeling slightly guilty, but well-fed and contented.

"There's beer in the fridge." Jake called from the living room, "Help yourself to one if you like."

"Nice! Thanks." she called back, "you want one too?"

"No." He was standing in the doorway now, "I'm going to get some work done. I've lost a lot of time lately."

"You sure?" Kat had seen the state of him after his transformation.

"Yeah, I really think I'm feeling okay. Actually, *really* okay now you ask." He smiled, "I guess all those long puppy-naps helped."

Kat opened the fridge to get a drink. Sapporo – fancy Japanese beer. *Good* choice. She lifted a sleekly shaped silver can from the fridge, opened it and took a long gulp. Oh, she needed that. The tension from earlier was starting to dissipate. Can in hand she wandered over to where Jake was busy drawing.

"What you working on? I know that the marketing guys are doing a push on *Princess Sparkles* in a few weeks."

"Yeah," Jake blew pencil dust off a rough sketch, "just a couple of dozen poses for some ads. Should have them done tonight."

Kat flopped down on the couch, "Ah that's fine. I'll bring them into the office on Monday. You think you'll be okay for a couple of hours in the morning? I'll pull a sickie and come back to dog-sit."

"Should be, just leave me a bone to chew." He chuckled, turning back to his desk and adjusted the desk lamp.

Kat laughed uneasily. She had just about got through the evening, but she was impressed at how well Jake had bounced back. She watched him happily drawing heroic poses of his Unicorn Princess and her friends for a while, then settled onto the couch with her book.

I could probably get used to this life, she mused – if it wasn't for this crazy werewolf thing. She vowed to look into that tomorrow, see if she could find out more.

CHAPTER 6

Monday 15-March 2021.

  Moonrise: 07:22. Set: 20:21. 4.5%
  Sunset: 18:09.

Kat's alarm sounded, snapping her awake from a dream that was already evaporating. She turned it off and peered over the 'pillow ridge of chastity'.

Jake was still there! He was awake, eyes wide open staring at the ceiling.

"I'm still here." he murmured. "Seven AM, still myself."

"That's got to be good." Kat enthused, up on one elbow. "Has it stopped?" Jake was laying flat, corpse-like. He turned his head and made a half-smile.

"I'm not sure. My head's pounding. I think it means the change is near."

"But why haven't you changed yet? Last time must have been much earlier, when I was still sleeping." Kat flopped back, her head sunk into the pillow.

"Well, we know it's not about the sunrise, and it's not the full moon." Jake paused to think some more "But folk lore always connects werewolves with the moon. Even if the stories are made up, this…" he gestured vaguely at his body "is all real." His arm flopped weakly back to the bed.

"So, you think there might be something to the old fairy tales?" Kat was back up on her elbow.

"Yeah, I do. A lot of them are based somewhere on

a cautionary tale, something fanciful to help warn later generations. I reckon there *is* some connection to the moon." Then, he gasped "Of course!" He turned to face Kat, hurling the pillow between them away so that he could see her face "It makes sense. It's the *rising* and *setting* of the moon! It happens at different times of the day, even if you can't always see it in the daylight, it's still there."

"Brilliant! What time does the moon rise today?" Kat asked, excited. Jake turned over and grabbed his phone from the bedside table. He prodded at it for a little while, and looked up at Kat, face ashen in the light of the little screen.

"Seven twenty-two. It's Seven seventeen, we have under five minutes." He felt his stomach drop as if in freefall. It was all going to happen again.

"Shit, that's not long. Quick, what time does it set?" Kat sat bolt upright, heart racing.

"Eight twenty-one this evening." He sat up too, facing her. She put her hand round his and squeezed.

"It's okay, at least we know what's going to happen. The worst part, at least for me, was not knowing what was going on or where you were."

Jake let out a slow breath, trying to calm himself, prepare for what was about to happen. He could feel the pressure in his head building further. The breathing was helping, his anxiety levels seemed to be lowering and despite the pounding of his head, a sense of calm was beginning to flow over him.

Kat had moved away a little now, kneeling on the bed, watching Jake's chest slowly rise and fall, his eyes closed. They sat there for a little longer, there wasn't really much to say or do but wait and see what would happen.

Without warning, Jake doubled over in pain, Kat instinctively reached out an arm towards him "Aghh. No, it's fine, it doesn't hurt that bad..." He stopped to breathe, "... see you again at eight twen–" He stopped, head pulled down, then snapped back. The golden mist burst out from his skin in all directions, forming streams that writhed and dissolved into the air as they poured outwards. Jets of it billowed from the sleeves and neck of his t-shirt which began to sag as he lost mass.

The surface of his body started to blur like silt disturbed in water. The whole process happened in an almost eerie silence, until as abruptly as it began, the last of the mist evaporated into the air and was gone.

What remained, was of course Jake, but now transformed into a young dog. No longer the puppy, he looked maybe a year old now glossy golden coat, panting, showing strong, healthy white teeth and clear hazel brown eyes.

Comically, he was still more or less wearing the t-shirt from before. He tried to get up, but found himself tangled in the shorts too.

Kat helped him out of the redundant clothing and Jake licked her face, perhaps in thanks, his strong tail wagging happily.

"It's amazing." Kat said, holding him under the chin, "You really *are* getting bigger."

Although still unnerving, Kat was thankful that at least Jake's transformation hadn't resembled some tacky 80's horror movie with the wax melting flesh effects that were so popular at the time.

"Is this how it's going to be from now?" she said to Jake. Well, at least the puppy, no, DOG now had a name. "Can you understand me? Are you still in there?" Jake looked at her and cocked his head "Jake?" She repeated, hopefully. He twisted around and started chewing at his tail. *No, perhaps not then.*

A large mug of Jake's fancy coffee just about prepared Kat for what was going to be a difficult day ahead, but she'd faced plenty of hard days in her life and she'd gotten through them.

She looked down at Jake as he lay on a now rather undersized soft dog bed. "Can't leave you locked in the bathroom now. You're a little big for that." She crouched down to look him in the face. He opened one eye lazily "But I've got to go into work to bring your artwork to Jerome." She smiled to herself. *Bring your artwork to Jerome* Ha! I'm talking to a dog. She got up briskly, grabbed the portfolio with the new art that Jake had left for her, "Okay pup – be good, I'll only be a couple of hours. I'll pull a sickie and do some work from here this afternoon."

Jake closed his eye and got back to his nap.

Half an hour later, Kat knocked on Jerome's office door. Behind her, the quiet buzz of work went on in the large open-plan studio. She realised that she missed the sound of people, she'd been more or less alone for... had it only been a couple of days? Wow, it felt like a week.

The door opened and Jerome appeared. "Sorry to

keep you," He echoed into the ridiculously large mug he had to his face. "Japanese printers again, something about the wrong kind of paper." He eyed the portfolio, "That the *Sparkles* poses I asked for?"

Kat nodded and laid the large leather folio on a big empty table, unzipped it and spread out the papers.

"Ah, these look good." He moved closer, pulling his glasses up onto his wrinkled forehead and squinted. "How's Jake now? Bloody embarrassing with that no-show on Saturday."

Kat had to think on her feet, she hadn't considered what she was going to tell Jerome, "He's um– resting at the moment, had to pull an all-nighter to do these, dog-tired." She looked at her feet then shuffled the papers together.

"So, what happened on Saturday?" he asked, serious now.

"Personal matters." Kat ventured. Vague, sure, but it was believable. There had been a couple of times when Jake had turned work in a day or two late when he was feeling depressed.

"Okay," Jerome sighed, "tortured genius, I get it." He took another slurp from his coffee. "Best get these into finishing then Akiko needs them by Wednesday for the cherry blossom promotions."

"No problem, I've asked Mario to scan and pass them to Clive to colour." She set the cute unicorn princess drawings aside and pulled out the pages for the latest episode of *The Rising Flesh*. Jerome's face lit up.

"Ooh, now this is what I've *really* been waiting for." He enthused.

"Um, yeah, about that..." Kat said in a small voice.

Jerome could be seen through the glass partition for the next hour pacing his office dialling and re-dialling Jake's number. As soon as he'd finished reading, Kat saw meerkat-heads pop up and down outside from behind monitors in response to Jerome's anguished cry then slipped quietly back to her desk.

By the time Jerome had gone worryingly quiet in his office, Kat had been able to sort out most of the important things on her task-list for the week, and delegate a few others on the strength of letting on (*just between us, okay*) what had upset Jerome so much. Gossip was HARD CURRENCY in an office like this.

She popped her head gingerly around the door of the boss's office "Jerome? Hi, um I need to head off for the rest of the day... Um, women's things." She knew that he wouldn't want to quiz her on that, but she let him know that she'd taken care of her work and had some schedule data to work on at home if she felt better. "I'll drop in on Jake if I can." She fibbed.

"Okay. Yes, that would be *lovely*." Came the measured reply "If he could perhaps give me a call, you know, when he's *feeling better*... perhaps we can talk a little about plotlines?" A breath, *calm, think of the cherry fucking blossoms...*

The metal food bowl in the kitchen clattered and rang then Jake came bounding out of the kitchen to greet Kat before she'd even closed the apartment door. She bumped it closed, sat on the floor and let him jump all over her, licking her face.

"Ohhh, you're a good boy. Did you miss me?"

Jake backed up, sat neatly "YUF".

Kat's eyes opened wide "Did you just speak to me?" she gasped.

"YUF" Jake's tail was wagging furiously, polishing the already spotless marble floor tiles.

Kat's nose wrinkled; something didn't smell good. "Uh, oh. Have you been a stinky puppy?" she cooed.

Jake got to his feet, scampered to the kitchen and waited at the doorway, looking back at Kat. She followed into the kitchen.

It wasn't pretty, but at least he'd used the big absorbent training pad she'd left for him.

"Well, I guess house-training a neat-freak werewolf isn't going to be so tough," she laughed. Jake panted and wagged his tail while Kat cleaned up and replaced the pad.

A little later, Kat was standing in the living room, putting off calling Officer Poole. She had to tell her something so that they wouldn't come back with more questions. Before, she'd *wanted* them to investigate, but now... well, God only knows what would happen if they found out what *really* happened.

She found herself absent-mindedly running her eye along a set of floating glass shelves. Carefully ordered along them were rows of beautifully detailed resin figures – characters from Jake's graphic novels. Pride of place in the centre of the middle shelf was the ill-fated Michelle from *The Rising Flesh*, brandishing her trademark bone saws. The other main characters flanked her on both sides with a couple of zombies at the ends for good measure.

Below that, painted in gaudy purple, *Princess Sparkles*

and her multi-coloured friends pranced in a neat row. Suddenly, Kat couldn't help feeling she was looking at an oversized and incredibly odd set of chess pieces – in all this time, she'd not seen it before. Two sides of a chess board, both very different worlds, both born of the beautiful brain of the guy... where was he? Ah yes, that gentle, brilliant guy who was currently under the coffee table licking his– ugh, that's not a good look.

"Okay, let's do this." She muttered to herself. She'd put Poole's direct number in her contacts so there really was no excuse not to call her. The line rang a couple of times, then.

"Alice Poole, hello?"

"Oh, hi. Um, it's Kat Benson from the other day. Missing person report?" she began nervously. Shit, she was going to have to *lie* to the police.

"Ah, Miss Benson. How can I help? Are you holding up okay?"

"Yes. Yes, I'm fine, thanks. Actually, I've got some good news." She was pacing, Jake had completed his canine ablutions and was watching her intently. "Yes, uh, Jake's back, and he's fine."

"Oh, that's very good to hear." Poole said, "What happened to him?" Kat froze for a moment.

Then it came to her; a detail that she'd overlooked while looking in the lift lobby the other night. The door next to the lift. It was marked 'rooftop'. "Yeah, uh. It seems that he had one of his little meltdown things and ended up hiding in the little garden space up on the roof. Nobody ever goes there and I just didn't think to look up there."

"Well, that explains a lot." Poole said, sounding

relieved. "Can you pass him to me, I'd like to ask him a couple of questions, just to make sure he's okay."

Well, that's torn it, Kat thought.

"He, uh, he's resting at the moment. It's all been a bit much for him. Can he call you in the morning?"

"Sure, that's fine Miss Benson. Glad to hear it's all wrapped up. Can I help with anything else?"

Kat told her that was all, thanked the officer and hung up the phone. She sat shakily down on the couch. Jake came out from underneath the table and laid his chin on her knee, looking up at her.

"I think we may just have gotten away with it." she said. Jake tapped the floor a couple of times with his tail in uncertain agreement.

Kat closed her laptop with a satisfied grunt. A day's work done, dinner made, dog fed – hell, she'd even washed up and put everything away.

She had been tweaking some staff schedules to pass a little time before Jake's transformation. He was laying on the floor, back pressed against her feet. Beside her, a white fluffy dressing gown, ready for Jake and a big glass of cold water on the coffee table. Jake's collar was off and lay beside it – she wasn't going to be caught out again.

Just a couple of minutes to go. She stroked Jake and rubbed behind his ear. He shifted and looked up at her contentedly.

"It's almost time, Jake. You want to get up now?" He huffed gently and climbed up onto the couch to sit next to her. He leaned into her and put his chin on her shoulder. Kat hugged him "You *do* make a good dog

Jake, you know that?"

Jake shook his head and whimpered softly. It was beginning. Kat moved back to the side of the couch to give him a little space.

Again, the golden mist streamed from the air, wrapping itself around the growing form within, and before she knew it, it was done, with surprisingly little drama.

Jake was left sitting on the couch, knees pulled up towards his body. Kat draped the dressing gown over him and offered him the water.

"Thanks Kat." he croaked, cleared his throat, "That was a lot less painful," he continued, with a much clearer voice.

"I could tell," she agreed, "do you think you'd ever get used to this?"

"I doubt it," he sipped his water and put the dressing gown on properly, tying the belt thoughtfully, "It's playing hell with my day. And don't forget, the time's going to keep shifting."

"That's true, how are you going to keep working?"

"I guess dogs sleep most of the day, so that's what I've been trying today. I can work tonight again."

"That's not much of a life." Kat said sadly. His hand was on the couch and she put hers on top of his. His deep hazel eyes were constant between his transformations, she noticed.

"Well, to be honest, it's just been work and sleep for me for the last couple of years anyhow, so I guess it's not a lot of difference."

"It's not right." Kat shook her head, "I'm going to look into this, see if I can find out more about it."

"What, on the internet?" he scoffed, "It'll be FULL of nutters claiming to be The Wolf-Man, vampires and the rest."

"I know," Kat said, "but I've *got* to at least try."

"Something interesting," he began. He turned his hand palm-upwards and squeezed hers back. "I can remember a lot from today."

Kat brightened "Really? That's fantastic."

"Yes, it's still a lot like a dream but there are moments of clarity. I can remember you talking to me and desperately wanting to talk back to you."

She took his hand in both of hers and held it, "I noticed! You *did* try, I thought I was just imagining it."

"We should work on that... will you stay again tonight?" he looked down, shy suddenly.

"Of course, Jake. I want to help you, I really do." She paused a moment, gathering up a thought that had been lingering in the back of her mind for most of the afternoon, "Can we try something? I know you might not agree at first, but I think it's probably important."

He looked at her quizzically, "Sure, what's on your mind?"

Kat drew her breath, "Well, as a dog, you're getting to be nearly fully grown, and I know it's not healthy for a dog to be cooped up in the house all day long." Jake sensed where she was going with this and stiffened. Kat held on tightly to his hand and ploughed on, "I know, I know but a dog needs to have exercise. We could just try a couple of minutes at the park, just to see how we get along."

Jake sighed deeply, "You're right, I know. Just go easy eh?"

"That's great Jake. It'll be so good for you."

"How do you do it?" Jake asked.

"Do what?" She cocked her head, searching his eyes.

"This. I mean, how do you just go back to *normal* things like walks in the park, going to work after seeing what you just saw – twice now?" He took a ragged breath. Kat put a hand on his arm to comfort him.

"I know what you mean. I just guess it's what I do. I had to face up to some pretty awful crap when I was growing up. Things were pretty bad with my dad and what he did to mum..." she stared off into the distance as she recalled those dark times. Jake put his hand onto hers. "I didn't really have a choice but to get on with things. I couldn't just get up and leave, I had nowhere to go, not a lot of friends I could be with. Perhaps everyday things are my coping mechanism."

She leant over and hugged him. She could feel him hesitate for a moment as she realised that he was uncomfortable about being touched, but before she had finished the thought, he relaxed into her, arms pinned slightly awkwardly to his sides.

Kat broke away, coughed; had she overstepped a boundary? "You hungry?" she asked changing the topic.

"Uh, nah I'm fine those biscuits earlier were enough."

"You remember?" Kat was excited again – then, "How were they?"

Jake chuckled, "They seemed great at the time." He closed his eyes, trying to remember, "Best thing I'd ever tasted if I recall."

"You certainly wolfed them dow– oh," she put her

hand to her mouth, "Sorry, not a good choice of words."

"Don't worry about it," he smiled, "I'm gonna go take a shower and get dressed. Need to get to work."

"What you working on now?" Kat glanced over at the drawing board. It had some fresh paper clipped to it.

"Next series of *Rising Flesh*." He said mysteriously, "Well *last* series, truth be told."

"You've got to talk with Jerome about that," she pleaded, "he was absolutely LIVID when he saw how you ended the last series."

"Don't worry," he said over his shoulder, "I've got a great storyline."

"But you killed off Michelle!" she shouted after him. "How can you have *Rising Flesh* without Michelle?" The reply, came there none save for the sound of the shower running.

When Jake returned smelling as well as looking fully human again Kat was curled up on the couch with her laptop.

"You still working?" he asked, peering over her shoulder from behind the couch.

"Nope. Seeing what I can find out about this werewolf thing." She gestured at her web browser which must have had twenty tabs open.

"Sheesh. You get anywhere?" he asked leaning in to look at yet another badly designed conspiracy site. Nestled amongst the mainly unsavoury ads were claims that assorted celebrities were werewolves or vampires. One link promised a heated debate on video as to whether a certain gender-fluid game-show host was a succubus or an incubus.

"So, not much luck then." he said shaking his head, rounding the couch to the other end of the room.

"No," she mumbled, opening another link, "been at it a couple of hours solid today, just the usual nonsense..." she drifted off as a page caught her attention. In the background, Kat heard Jake adjusting his chair, the lamp click on and the rattle of pencils being selected from a silver tin.

The next hour was filled with the sounds of keys tapping and pencil scratches as the pair quietly engrossed themselves in their projects.

Kat was the first to break the silence.

"I think I might have something." She spoke slowly, doubt still in her voice.

"Aliens?" Jake mocked without looking up. His double-spread comic page was now filled with a rough layout. He carefully unclipped the newspaper sized sheet and added a new, fresh page.

"Not this time." she replied, typing furiously now. "It's a forum site. I almost missed it."

"How come?" Jake was stretching before starting his next page.

"It's really low-key. Not full of ads, pop-ups, hardly any other sites linking into it." She looked up at Jake, who had stopped to listen. "Not hiding as such, but this site's not trying to attract a lot of attention."

"So, what's on there?" He was behind her again. The page was an ugly, drab olive colour, no flashy graphics at all.

"Forum, discord chat – the usual stuff. I've signed

up and posted a question."

"What?!" Jake burst out, "Are you mad? That place is going to be full of dangerous nutters!"

"Don't worry, I used a fake name and a hotmail account. I'm not stupid."

"Okay, sorry. What did you ask?"

She clicked on the forum titled 'Reporting new phenomena'

> From: Suzy1997
> My boyfriend has suddenly become a werewolf. What can I do about it?
> [views: 19, replies: 0]

"Boyfriend?" asked Jake "*That's* a new phenomena."

Kat blushed, "Um, yeah like I said fake name and stuff." *Shit, shit shit what was I thinking.* But Jake didn't seem to have taken it badly.

"That's a lot of views so soon for a crappy little site like this – look, there's only a couple of dozen posts in that topic. Doesn't look like they get a lot of visitors, so who's reading this?"

The moment he finished speaking, the laptop chimed. At the top of the page, '(1) New Personal Messages' had appeared.

"We got a hit." said Kat. "Like you say, some nutter or sex-pest." She clicked to open the message.

> From: CrystalEnergy72 [ADMIN]
> Subject: New Werewolf.
> Hello Suzy1997,
> Tell me more about your new werewolf! When did it start happening? Did you see him transform?

"Not a lot to go on there, though this guy's an admin,

not just some random whacko, so that ought to count for something." Kat surmised.

"I wouldn't count on it" Jake was still very sceptical. "Still, write back, see how it goes."

Kat clicked on 'reply' and typed.

From: Suzy1997
Hi CrystalEnergy,
It started a few days ago and yes I saw the transformation both ways a couple of times now. What's happening? How can we make it stop?

A minute passed, then:

From: CrystalEnergy72 [ADMIN]
Must have been scary, all that twisting and tearing flesh - John Carpenter stuff, am I right?

Kat replied

From: Suzy1997
Actually, it was sort of beautiful in it's own strange way. Like a golden cloud of mist.

The reply came straight back.

From: CrystalEnergy72 [ADMIN]
Suzy. Okay, now I'm being totally serious. All that horror movie stuff just then was a bit of a test. So, tell me. He first appeared as a puppy, didn't he?

Jake and Kat turned to look at each other, mouths wide open.

"Holy crap!" Jake gasped, "I think this guy's genuine."

CHAPTER 7

Tuesday 16-March 2021.

  Moonrise: 07:36. Set: 21:30. (9.4%)
  Sunset: 18:11.

6:45: Two phones buzzed and jingled on their respective bedside tables. Kat stretched, fumbled for hers, dismissed the alarm. *God, this bed's comfy* she thought. And even with the pillow division, her side still felt bigger than the rickety little one back at her apartment.

Jake had turned his phone off before Kat. She turned around to see him sitting up tapping at the screen.

"Morning. You sleep okay?" he asked without looking up.

"Mmmm... Yes, like a log. What you doing?" She sat up and peered over his shoulder at the screen. He smelled warm, comfy. She leaned her head on his shoulder; she could happily sit like this all morning.

"I've found an astronomy app that lets you know when the moon and things are visible in the sky. Seven thirty-six this morning."

"Oh, that's handy. Show me later, and I'll put it on my phone too."

"No problem, hang on, I'll send you an invite to download." He tapped a couple of times, then Kat's phone chimed.

"Ta. I'll set it up after breakfast." She was far too comfy to move now. "You want me to sort out some dinner tonight? It's going to be a little late when you're back again."

"Um. Nine thirty, according to this. No, I should be okay with some biscuits when you eat." He patted his tummy, "I think I'm losing a little weight."

Kat chuckled and pinched his belly, it tickled and he squirmed "God, Jake you're not *fat*."

Jake fell silent for a moment, "Feels like it. Stuck in this apartment all day every day, I hardly get any exercise."

He got out of bed quickly. Kat almost fell across the pillows, "Don't forget to set your location and a ten minute advance warning." He paused, considering something of vital importance. Kat looked up to see what had made him stop to think. "I'm gonna try to go to the loo *before* the transformation. Should save you some trouble later." He smiled and closed the bathroom door.

Kat flopped back on the bed. "Pfft" she realised that she was a little miffed that he'd gotten up out of bed while she was enjoying a little snuggle, but hey, saving her from cleaning up his poop – *that's* considerate.

"Thought it would be easier if I just wore my bathrobe." Jake announced. He'd smelled toast and coffee in the kitchen and came to investigate.

"Don't forget to take your arms out of the sleeves first." Kat looked up from buttering some toast "What you want on yours?"

Jake was plucking experimentally at the fluffy white sleeves of his robe "Um, Marmite please."

Kat pulled a face, "Ugh, really?"

"Yup," Jake opened a cupboard and pulled out a couple of mugs "It's got loads of B vitamins in it, might be good for depression." He carefully pushed down the coffee plunger and poured.

"No, honestly there's been quite a bit of research into it." He sipped the coffee, nodded approvingly and handed a mug to Kat.

"Sounds like hokum," she scoffed.

"Ha!" he laughed, "I think we're past hokum and out the other side with all this crazy doggy stuff."

"Yeah, I guess so." Kat handed him his toast and pulled up a stool to the breakfast bar. "Oh, we've got to call Poole this morning, or rather *you* need to." She bit into her buttered toast – no jam in Jake's kitchen, "I called yesterday to say you were back but they need to hear it from you."

She explained the story that she'd made up so that at least they could be consistent.

Jake fished his phone out of the deep pockets of the robe and copied the number from Kat's proffered phone.

Kat munched her toast while Jake recounted a very believable rendition of their cover story to Officer Poole.

"And, Case Closed." Jake said, placing his phone on the counter. "Good toast." he added, winking. Kat smiled; whatever was happening, Jake was looking and sounding so much more confident than she'd ever seen him.

Jake's phone chimed. "MMm–" He swallowed the coffee in his mouth, "Three minute warning. I wonder, should I really finish this coffee? You don't want a hyper dog on your hands all day."

"Ah, should be okay, we'll run it off at the park, remember?" She offered her mug up to toast with. Jake obliged, clinking mugs, then downed the remainder.

"I'm not going to lie," he started, "the idea still terrifies me. I don't even know if I'd be in control. It's really hard to remember stuff when I'm in dog form."

Kat nodded. "Don't worry, I promise to take it easy. We'll try walking a little way up the street. If you're fine with that then the park should be a – well, a walk in the park."

"Okay, then; let's see how we get on... Ah, okay," he winced, "It's starting."

Kat put her mug down and stepped over to help. "Don't forget to take your arms out of the sleeves."

"Ugh.... Okay, you said." He shuffled his arms inside the robe.

"Where do you want to change, living room, bedroom?" Kat followed him, toast in hand as he staggered a little.

"Crap... Agh, um, I hadn't thought of that." He moved out of the kitchen through to the living room and stopped. "Ah, okay, looks like it's going to be... Here," he sat down on the floor, leaning against the couch. "Half nine, okay?"

Kat nodded, "Yep, I'll be ready. See you later." She planted a kiss on his forehead just as the golden mist began to billow out of his robe.

Jake's vision blurred. A wave of pain flowed out from the core of his body to his skin, where it turned to an itching sensation. Another wave burst though him, and ended in a warm numbness.

It's happening again, the moon, it's rising above the horizon. Something is different in me, something that makes me change like this, something... Can't find the word, can't find the thinking, the... Scared thoughts in me, run away, legs can't run, fight the frightening thing, fight it, bite it, make it go, bark at it, away, go!

It's going, look at me, I'm strong, I made it go, I can protect, must protect... Who? Where is she, I'm lost, trapped in white, soft dig, dig out, find the one I must protect.

Kat set her toast down on the coffee table and pulled the struggling Jake from out of the robe. He barked and leapt, licking her face, wagging his tail. He was fully grown now, a magnificent golden retriever. Kat hugged him, and scratched him behind his ears, ran her fingers through his soft fur.

"Oh, Jake just look at you, you're beautiful!" She had a tear forming in her eye. At first, the transformation had been the stuff of nightmares, but this time she was able to see it differently; it was breath-taking, magical.

"Okay, my wonderful boy, we're going to have such a day today."

Kat's phone rang shattering the moment. It was Jerome. Unusual for him to call at this hour.

"Hey, Jerome. What's up?"

"Kat, SO sorry for calling you this early. I've done a dumb thing. Those schedules you sent to me, I've deleted them." He sounded genuinely embarrassed.

Kat rolled her eyes and snuck a bite of her breakfast, "That's okay, I've got them on my laptop. I'll email them to you in a moment." In the background, Jake had found a ball which had rolled under the couch. He barked at it. "Jake!" she called. Then coughed; a toast crumb had gotten lodged. "Sorry..." she gave one last cough, "toast crumb."

"Oh..." Jerome reacted, surprised, "You're at Jake's? For *breakfast*?"

"Uh, yes. I'm... Helping with his dog," she lied.

"Okayy." Jerome intoned, dubiously, "Can I talk with him for a moment? He's not been answering his phone for the last couple of days."

"Oh," this caught her off guard, "He's, changing right now." She thought for a moment, "Hey, Jerome? I've got a load of unused holiday. I know it's short notice but can I take the rest of this week off?"

Jerome thought for a second or two, "Okay, yes, I suppose. Debbie can cover for you." He mustered himself to ask what was now burning in his mind, "Kat? You and Jake aren't... Well, *an item* now are you?"

She spluttered, Jake stopped chewing the sleeve of his bathrobe and looked up, ears pricked.

"What?" she said unconvincingly, "whatever gave you that idea?"

Jerome wasn't going to press her on the matter so he said his goodbyes and hung up.

Jake was still looking at her intently, "What?" she cried plaintively, spreading her arms in mock affliction. "He's just jumping to conclusions. You know Jerome." Jake's eyes flicked to her hand, which was still holding the last of the toast.

"Oh, you just want my toast? You didn't hear what Jerome was saying?"

"YUF!" he was sitting up with his best 'I'm a good dog' pose. Kat threw him the crust and he deftly caught it, eagerly sniffing the rug afterwards for any dropped crumbs.

By mid-morning, Kat had given up looking for more information about Jake's condition online. Every link she followed was either a dead-end, some ghastly spam site or the occasional rather dubious 'niche' adult site. It really looked like that forum site from the other evening was the place to go.

She logged back in, there was a message waiting for her from CrystalEnergy72.

> **Sorry to contact you again. I would very much like to hear more. Was I right about the transfiguration to juvenile form?**
> **Please. Trust me, I have experience in these matters and I know that I can help you.**
> **Don't worry, I am not seeking payment of any kind. But you _DO_ need help with this.**

He was right, they were just about coping with this thing. Jake certainly couldn't do this alone, and what would the future hold? How could he go on with this in the long term? She would talk with Jake about this tonight.

But now. Time for an adventure.

The midday sun was bright, but in March in the UK it could be deceptive. Kat pulled out a purple fleece from her bag. As she did so, a crumpled piece of paper fell to the floor unnoticed.

"Jake! Walk time!" she shouted. No response. She

went into the living room and fished the collar and lead out. "Jake?" she called.

He was lying under the coffee table, trying to sink into the rug, hoping he could be invisible.

"It's okay, we're just going to the park, like we talked about." she said, down on her hands and knees. Jake whined feebly, chin pressed firmly to the floor. "We can get some chips for lunch!" she tried.

That worked. There's no way that a dog of that age, with no training could have known the word 'chips' perhaps the word filtered down to where the *human* side of Jake was buried and then back out to the hungry Labrador brain.

Jake scrabbled out from under the table and sat neatly, panting gently. The collar had to be extended to the absolute maximum to fit, but it seemed good enough. Kat ran through her checklist patting her pockets as she went, *doggie bags, phone, purse, keycard, keys.* Good to go.

Once more, at the outside lobby door, Jake paused uncertainly. Kat opened the door and the traffic sounds and noises of the city flooded in. Jake flinched.

Kat crouched down, "It's okay." she said softly, "I'm here with you. You're on your lead so nothing bad can happen to you."

He looked up at her and stood slowly, then peering nervously at the street outside, took a step forwards. "That's it, you can do it."

He sniffed, ears pulled back, tail tucked down between his legs. Another step. A couple more and he was at the door, nose sampling the crisp spring air.

"You're doing it. Remember, you were almost going

to go to London a week ago?" Jake took another step; he seemed to be building determination to do this. One more step... He was out. Kat stepped through the door after him and it closed softly behind them. He glanced back at the door, then up to Kat. There was no turning back now.

"Okay, it's just a short walk to the crossing, then after that we'll be almost at the park. Just keep to my side, close to the buildings."

They walked on, slowly, Jake's tail was still tucked in – a sure sign of fearfulness in any dog. A bus passed by, huge and noisy, casting a shadow on the pavement. Jake froze for a moment, then forged on.

Kat kept up the words of encouragement as they approached the crossing. They took up position on the textured paving stones in front of the crossing itself and Kat pushed the button to stop the traffic. Jake sat by her feet quietly until the traffic stopped. He jumped as the signal began beeping for them to cross.

A mother approached them from the other side as they walked over the road, her child, holding her hand firmly spotted Jake. "Mummy, look doggie!" Kat smiled at the pair as they got within a few feet. The child ran her hand along Jake's back, chortling with delight, "Lovely doggie, Mummy!"

At the pavement on the other side, Kat scratched Jake behind the ear "You *are* a lovely doggie, and I'm so proud of you. We're nearly there now."

They were a little under half way now, and Jake had picked up his pace to a normal walking speed. He seemed to be gaining a little confidence as they walked alongside the iron railings and sandstone posts of the park. Open swathes of grass could be glimpsed through gaps in the bushes and trees that lined the perimeter.

Rounding the stately entrance gates to the park, Jake stopped and looked up at Kat. His tail was raised and wagging gently. Ahead of them, lay the wide central path which ran through to the canal bridge and across to the far side.

"It's okay, Jake. You'll like the park. It's a safe place." She smiled at him and he wagged his tail slowly, still a little uncertain.

They passed a couple of joggers as they joined the main path from the smaller routes which wound their way between trees, bushes and quiet spaces.

Jake's head was up, sniffing the air, tail erect now and bobbing happily as he took in the surroundings. Kat had an idea. "You want to go off your lead, so you can explore?"

His tail said it all, wagging happily, ears pricked, "YUF!"

"Okay, you'll be safe, but stay close." She unclipped the lead and he bounded off.

Big place, green, wide. So big. Want to see it all, smell it all. So many smells. My lead is off, can I go? Can I see it all? Kat Lady is nodding, Kat Lady is safe, Jake is safe.

Such a big place, I want to run. Bark at Kat Lady, 'wait for me'.

I'm running, I'm so fast, so light, I'm strong. The grass whipping past my nose. I can smell all the smells as they dance and weave around me. I've never known a landscape of smells before, it's like a new colour in my mind. I've never run with four legs before, only two.

Remembering the time when Jake was not a dog. Jake was sad, all was inside, never outside.

HAPPY! Bark for the joy of being alive.

I've run so far. I can see Kat Lady, she's waving at me... She has a treat! Run to Kat Lady, run fast, fast.

Kat lady is happy, gives me a treat. Eat! More treats? Her hand smells of treats, more treat smells in her pocket. Want them. Bark!

Jake jumped up at Kat, tail wagging furiously. She crouched down to give him a huge hug. His nose was in her pocket in a flash rooting about for more treats.

"Wow, you really can run fast," she said in between face-licks, "I wasn't sure if you were going to run away forever."

He made a "huff" sound and put his paw on her knee, sat and looked deep into her eyes.

"Yes, I know you'd never do that." She gave him, another long hug. His fur was so soft, so warm, "Okay. Let's go find those chips." Jake barked in agreement wagging his big golden tail.

The chip van was parked near the North entrance to the park plying their usual lunchtime trade.

Kat sat on a bench, looking down the slope at the canal. Joggers, mothers with prams, workers out on their lunch-break passed by. Jake was sat next to her on the bench pushed up close. His tail had fallen through the open back of the bench and was idly swaying back and forth, accelerating each time a chip came his way.

This was how Kat often fantasised spending a spare afternoon with a partner; just sitting, watching the world go by. Her previous relationships had been brief and few. The guys she attracted seemed to think that her long blonde hair naturally pegged her as a bit easy, and that was tiresome. What the hell did that have to do with her bloody hair colour! Jake on the other hand, she thought, didn't really seem to have noticed. To him, she was 'Just Kat'. Dependable, reliable, unintimidating.

Was this the kind of life that she really wanted? She could do worse, just a girl and her dog. Except, of course Jake *wasn't* just a dog. It was far too easy to think of him that way right now, she was forgetting, there was a *person* inside there too.

The rest of the day was just as idyllic for Kat. Chilling out at Jake's apartment, watching his HUGE TV – there are times, when size is *everything*. Jake curled up at her feet. Once, he had a dream, feet twitching, little yelps and huffs. Kat stroked him and cooed in his ear until he settled again.

Before she knew it, her phone was chiming the time for Jake to return. She'd let him sleep for most of the early evening as she knew he'd want to work into the small hours.

She scratched him behind the ear, "Jake, time to wake up." He opened one eye and stretched, "It's nearly time to change."

Jake yawned and licked his chops, then sat up, looking a little sleepy. "You've had a busy day today. I'll go get your bath robe."

When she returned with the robe and a glass of water, he was sitting neatly on the couch. Kat took his collar off and slipped the robe over his shoulders.

"We're going to have to get you a new one of these."
She said tugging at the remaining adjustment loop.

Jake made a little yelp.

When it was all over, Jake was sitting hunched over on the couch. His brow beaded with sweat, panting a little as if he had run for a bus.

"How are you?" asked Kat, softly.

Jake paused for a moment to catch his breath, then threw his arms in the air "Absolutely, fucking amazing!" Kat was startled for a moment, then threw her arms around him. What a complete change from just a couple of nights ago.

"It was so vivid," he continued. Kat sat back to look at his face. He was beaming, "the park was *such* a good idea. I've never felt like that in my life." He grabbed both of Kat's hands. "I can remember it all, every moment."

"That's fantastic," Kat began, squeezing Jake's hands, "you should have seen yourself. Running, jumping."

"I know. And the most incredible thing was how the sense of smell works. I'd never realised, I thought that dogs just had a good sense of smell. No, it all ties together, it's like you can SEE scents."

"And you were *outside*, at last. After all those years of being trapped by your agoraphobia."

"Yes!" he almost shouted, "It's like one curse has dispelled the other." He stopped for a moment, "But *is* it really a curse, when I feel so good – so *alive*, so *awake*?"

Kat's eyes flicked down for an instant, "Um, mate you might want to do up your dressing gown," she smirked, looking away, "your little chappie there's also awake."

He looked down in horror, "Shit!" he hissed, pulled the robe tightly around himself and fled for the bedroom.

Jake slammed the door closed. Crap. *Oh, crap, I've made an utter tit of myself.* He grabbed a shirt and shorts from a drawer and clutched them tight in balled-up fists of frustration and embarrassment. *What's she going to think of me now? I've blown it... 'little', 'little' she said. Oh, God is that what she sees?* The metallic sting of anxiety burned in his stomach.

After showering, he sat on the bed, just breathing, getting a grip on himself. When he had calmed himself sufficiently he opened the bedroom door and peeped out.

The bedroom door slammed. She giggled to herself. *Easy mistake to make. But what a difference. Such an improvement, and oh this was the most happy I've seen him in... well, since I've known him.* She thought about the 'little slip' just now. *Cute,* she thought, *'unintimidating'* then *Hmmm, we need to go out and get a new collar tomorrow. We should make the park a regular thing.*

The bedroom door opened and Jake peeped out.

"Hey," Kat said brightly. "Better now? You want a beer or you just want your water?"

Jake approached the couch, eyes lowered. He sat and took the glass from Kat's hand.

"Thanks... about just now."

Kat waved dismissively, "Don't worry about it. Just one of those things."

Jake was blushing again, "Look, I'm sorry if I offended you. I didn't realise-" Kat put her finger to his lips.

"It's fine. Really. I understand." She whispered.

Jake sat back on the couch, "I think this might be a turning point in my life. I know I've said it before, but I really appreciate you sticking by me right now." From the big terrace windows, blue flickers of an emergency vehicle passing by momentarily lit up the edges of the frames.

Kat turned to face him, "I think we should go see that guy from the forum." she said suddenly, "He really does seem genuine."

"That guy?" Jake scoffed, "He's just some nutter off the internet. What does he know?"

"But the way he described your transformations." Kat implored, "How could he possibly know. It's too much of a coincidence, Jake. Besides, what else do we have to go on? We need to understand what's happening to you, how we're going to deal with this in the long term."

We, long term. Jake thought about that for a second. Were they a 'we'? It sounded so easy for her to say, so natural. Did they have a future together? Perhaps. It felt right somehow, it had always felt right when she had come over each week.

He looked up. Kat was standing by the window, her face edged with flickering blue light.

"Something's up." she said, peering into the darkness, "Not sure if it's police, or what."

"Can you see where they're going?" Jake asked, stepping up behind her. The warmth from her body made him realise how close he was standing to her – he had never done that. Before, he would have felt uncomfortable, just being this close to another person. "Let's take a look outside, maybe we can see."

Jake unlocked the endmost panel of the huge folding glass door and they stepped out onto the terrace.

Kat peered over the edge of the balcony, her hands gripping the cold stonework. "They're gone now." she said.

"No, look over to the right – see, across from where the park is." Kat squinted... yes, she could just about make out the occasional blue flash against the–

"Shit! Look, flames." she gasped, "I thought it was just the street lights making the sky orange."

Jake leaned out to get a better view, one foot off the ground. "Careful." Kat pressed her hand to his chest, "Don't fall." He leaned back, both feet planted firmly on the ground.

"Looks like it's coming from the industrial estate on the other side of the park."

"Whoa! That's really near to where I live."

"Close enough to spread, you think?"

Kat scoffed, "doubt it'll burn, with all the damp." She shivered, "Come on, let's get inside, It's getting cold."

The apartment was peaceful, busy scratchings from Jake's pencil, soft tapping of Kat's keyboard again.

Jake looked up from his drawing board in his own pool of light at Kat, her face illuminated by her laptop screen.

"You want to see how the next series of Rising Flesh begins?"

Kat jumped up from the couch, almost skidded to a halt at Jake's desk in her thick purple socks.

"Show me, show me!" she squealed.

Laid out, twice print-size was the first double-page spread of the graphic novel. Some of the lines were still a little rough and a handful of post-its littered the sheet with notes for sections to change, or ideas.

Gripping his shoulders, Kat scanned the page eagerly. The first, large pane showed Michelle, on top of the rusting train carriage swiping at the masked assailant with her bone saws, she over-reached and fell, seemingly to her doom.

But, as she fell, she grabbed the boot of her attacker, unbalancing them, pitching them over the edge and into the ravenous masses of undead below. Michelle found herself slipping over the edge to join him, losing her weapons, but managed to kick in the already cracked window. She swung herself inside the carriage to safety in a rain of glass. Below, the leader of the Silent Raiders group met a sticky, but just end.

"Yesss!" Kat hugged him from behind, "I knew you couldn't kill her off."

Jake smiled to himself, "See, I *do* know what I'm doing." he said.

"Clever boy!" she cooed into his neck, "You want a biscuit?"

Jake jerked alert, then realised he'd been pranked, he span around in his chair, "Hey! Not fair!"

"I've got something to tell you as well," she said, turning more serious, "I've been talking some more with that chap on the supernatural forum."

"Nutter."

"Maybe not. I think he really might have some answers for us."

Again, 'us' thought Jake, he felt an unfamiliar warmth spread through him.

"Okay, then," he conceded, "what's the plan?"

Kat switched into her *organiser* mode. "So: His name's Marcus, he runs the website which is essentially a front for a group that monitor and record supernatural activity. He says he's seen this before."

Jake looked at her suspiciously, "Go on..."

"We've talked a bit today, but to cut a long story short, I think we ought to go meet him."

"When?" Jake asked coldly, "And more importantly, where?" His pulse was beginning to race.

Kat laid a hand on his shoulder, she hoped it would come across as reassuring, "We could see him this weekend. Saturday night. It's only a half hour taxi ride away."

Jake's eyes narrowed in thought, "Hmmm, the taxi ride I reckon I can deal with." He sighed. "But it's going to be a real stretch to just go meet a random stranger." He dabbed at imagined sweat on his forehead.

Kat eyed, him, waiting for him to finish his train of thought, face eager, hands pressed together as if in prayer, "But...?"

"But," he echoed. "But I'll do it," he sighed, resigned.

Kat was already skidding back to the couch and began typing. She looked up and added, "He wants to see the transformation."

Jake gulped.

CHAPTER 8

Wednesday 17-March 2021.

Moonrise: 07:52. Set: 22:38. (15.8%)
Sunset: 18:13.

THE MORNING TRANSFORMATIONS were happening a little later each day as the cycle of the moon progressed. This gave time for a more relaxed schedule in the morning.

"Morning briefing." said Kat smartly, setting a mug of hot, dark coffee on the kitchen counter.

Jake's hair was a bit of a mess, he looked tired but his eyes still sparkled with energy. "Yessir, Sargent Benson Sir." He quipped, eyeing the toast Kat had made. Too much Marmite – only a true Marmite lover knew the right amount to put on, he mused. But he appreciated the gesture nonetheless.

"Dog-time oh-seven fifty-two till twenty-two thirty-eight." She even had a notebook with this all written down.

"Check." Jake went along with it cheerfully, but Kat couldn't hold a straight face any longer.

"Okay, okay," she relented, "anyhow. I need to get back home to grab a few more things. You want to come along for the walk through the park?"

Jake's eyebrows shot up over the big mug, "Yeah! Sure!" he realised that he was overreacting a little, then nonchalantly, "If you want the company, sure, park would be nice." He chewed his toast thoughtfully,

"So, you're moving in by stealth then?" he grinned, all big white teeth.

"Ha, looks like it buddy! You're stuck with me for a bit until we get a handle on this..." she made a little paws and panting tongue expression, "whatever it is."

With breakfast done, Jake went off to the bedroom to get ready for the daily transformation. A few minutes later, Kat heard barking from the bedroom – Jake had closed the door behind himself on the way in but forgotten that he wouldn't be able to open the door afterwards.

Kat opened the door to a slightly ashamed looking dog. "To be honest," she chuckled, "I'd probably have done the same thing."

Jake made a "Huff" sound and trotted out to the living room and took up position on the rug under the coffee table.

Outside, the rain began to lash against the wide expanse of glass. Kat peered outside as the sheen of water on the terrace boiled with raindrops, like TV static. "I think," she called over her shoulder, "we'll go out a little later."

Jake and Kat spent the morning playing tug with his dinosaur toy, a raucous game with an old towel and finally ending up sitting together on the rug between the couch and the table watching junk TV.

At last, the rain subsided and the clouds lightened a little.

"Looks like it's safe to go out now." Kat said to Jake. He was sleeping, head in her lap, the absolute epitome of comfort. His ears pricked up and he leapt to his feet, tail thrashing in expectation.

"Give me a minute to get ready and we'll be off." She called back on her way to the bedroom. Jake watched her disappear into the side corridor that led to the bedroom, still wagging his tail happily.

The weather was still a little gloomy and it was threatening to rain again, but that didn't dampen Jake's spirits as he charged back and forth along the path at the park.

Kat followed along, with her empty bag over her shoulder. The trees were starting to put out their spring leaves which they rustled proudly in the gathering breeze.

Jake was sniffing at the base of a tree when Kat got to the bridge. "Jake, let's go!" she called. His head popped up and he belted, full speed across the grass, paws thundering like a race-horse. The sound changed to the skittering of claws over the pavement as he joined her panting, tail high like a flag.

"You've totally got the hang of this dog stuff now haven't you," she said, tossing him a treat from her pocket. He caught it neatly and trotted ahead onto the bridge crunching loudly for a few seconds.

The canal lay beneath them, grey-green under the dirty clouds. The section that ran through the park was perfectly straight. From the middle of the bridge it was just about possible to make out where the waterway left the city and broke into the countryside beyond.

The wind changed suddenly and brought the acrid whiff of old smoke from last night's fire.

Jake had stopped at the far side of the bridge to wait for Kat. She caught up with him and held out the lead, "We need to go out the gate there." She pointed to the place where the main path branched off and passed through an arch of trees. "That's my street." A hollow laugh, "You'd think that a park-side apartment would be pretty fancy wouldn't you?"

Jake seemed to nod, "Huff." he vocalised.

"Pretty scabby on the East side of the canal." The wind blew more damp fumes from the unseen site.

Kat clipped the lead on and they set off towards the gate and the road beyond.

The first thing Kat saw was the blue and white police tape stretched across the road half way between them and her– *her building*. Gutted by fire, all the windows facing the road bar the ground floor, hollow, blackened; the roof above the fourth floor, a skeleton of burned timbers.

The street was empty, it was a cul-de-sac ending with rubbish-strewn railings bordering the industrial estate. Bits of plastic hanging from the metal spikes waved in the wind like ghosts, the only sound their fluttering, and the crunch of detritus under Kat's feet as she walked slowly down the middle of the road towards the fluttering blue tape.

Suddenly, she found herself pitched to the ground, she turned her ankle on an unseen piece of wreckage, landing hard on her hands.

Jake jumped to her side, fussing and whining; she looked at her hands, blackened from the oil and grime on the road, cut and beginning to bleed. The pain hadn't fully registered yet, so numb was she from the discovery that her home had gone.

A sound made her start. It was the door of the car parked behind her. A figure jumped out and ambled towards her, offering a hand to help her up. The old man saw her hands and helped her to her feet, by her arms. He was strong for an old man.

As she came to her senses, she recognised him.

"Mr Rudd?" she breathed, wincing; the cuts on her hands were beginning to sting sharply. She took a step towards him to look at him better, her knee hurt too. Jake continued to whine by her side, confused, frightened. She rubbed behind his ear soothingly with her knuckles, "It's okay, Jake, I'm okay... Kind of."

"Miss Benson, look at you you're bleeding. Quick, come to my car I have a first aid kit." He backed up towards the small red car, beckoning.

Kat followed, onto the pavement and sat on the worn stone steps of the shabby town house near the car. Jake followed, lead trailing behind. He sat in font of her with his chin on her knee whining.

Mr Rudd could be heard rummaging about in his car, muttering to himself. He stopped, seeming to have found what he was looking for. The door slammed shut and he sat beside Kat, laying out the things he'd gathered.

"Oh, dear, this looks nasty," he muttered. "Let me clean it up for you, are you okay?"

Kat nodded, a little dazed, "What happened? The Fire?" She looked towards the shell of her home, winced as Mr Rudd slowly poured water from a plastic bottle onto her cuts.

"It was terrible," he sighed, "the fire, it came from

old Mr Preston's flat so I'm told."

"But it was empty, he died months ago." The gravel and grime had mostly washed away. Mr Rudd produced a roll of paper kitchen towels and began gently dabbing at her palms. The pain wasn't quite so bad now.

"Indeed." He examined Kat's wounds, checking for any bits of gravel stuck in the cuts, "The police are treating it as suspicious. Want to talk with everyone that was there that night."

"I was away," she said in a faraway voice, still staring at the ruined building, "looking after a friend." Jake nuzzled under her arm with a little whine.

"You were lucky, girl." He opened a green plastic box and began rummaging about. "We barely got out." He stopped, watery eyes fixing hers, "Mrs Wilkins. She didn't."

"What! She died?" She stared down the street, "But she was on the ground floor, it's not burned."

"The smoke. It still got to her." he said sadly, "Don't forget why she lived on the ground floor my dear. She just didn't get out in time."

A tear fell down her cheek, Kat was trembling. "... and her cats?" but she knew. Mr Rudd shook his head sadly.

"Hold still, this might sting a little." Rudd opened a tube of antiseptic cream. "It looked a lot worse than it was, you've only got a few little cuts." He dabbed it onto the cleaned areas with the corner of a paper towel. Kat didn't notice the sting, "A little blood goes a long way." he said. There was a haunted tone to his voice.

"How come you were here, just now?" Kat asked. Rudd opened a plaster and began smoothing it onto her palm.

"Nowhere else to go yet. I was sleeping in my car." He opened another plaster, "I'll drive up to my sister's at the weekend," he feigned cheerfulness, "stay there until I get myself straight." He stopped to examine his work and nodded, satisfied. "She's in Portugal, you know. Nice this time of year, not too hot."

Kat flexed her fingers experimentally, "Thank you Mr Rudd–"

"Winston, call me Winston. You should get that checked out properly when you can. Don't get an infection."

Jake climbed up to the step where Kat was sitting and licked her face.

"That's a good, loyal dog you have there," Rudd said, smiling, "It's clear he really loves you."

Kat turned to look at Jake; he was panting, wagging his tail. She hugged him. "You have no idea, Mr Rudd – sorry, Winston." She looked back to the old man, "So. That's it then? We're all out on the street?"

Winston nodded slowly. "I'm afraid so Miss Benson, there's no sign of Mr Singh, and of course you saw his letter to the tenants. He's not going to be rebuilding of course. So... Yes, that's it."

Kat looked confused for a moment, then "The letter? Oh, I saw it but I didn't read it."

"You should, if you have it still." Winston replied. He was shaking, a little; angry but it didn't show in his voice.

"I'd better get back to– to my friend's house." said

Kat, standing slightly unsteadily at first. Winston thrust out his hand to catch her and helped her off the step. "Thank you, thank you so much." Her knee was still a little painful, but the gravity of the situation was beginning to hit home. It weighed in her stomach. Jake jumped down from the steps and stood, looking up at her, his tail down, ears back.

"I think he understands," Winston noted.

Kat hurried inside and threw herself onto the couch in floods of tears. She was crying for poor Mrs Wilkins, her dear little cats, Mr Rudd sleeping in his car with nobody to turn to. What had become of the other three tenants she may never know. At last, she cried for herself, homeless also, scared of being lost and alone. She didn't own many things that she cared especially for but all those little things added up to a life, and they were all burned – lost forever. The way that Winston had talked, he seemed to think that their landlord had something to do with the fire.

Jake nudged her elbow and whined. She looked over at him with reddened eyed and smiled through streaming tears. He jumped up onto the couch and curled himself against her, nose pressed firmly into the warmth under her arm.

"What am I going to do, Jake?" she sniffled. He whined, and slowly flapped his tail against her leg. "Everything is gone, you're all I have in the world that makes sense any more." She stroked the back of his head, "Hurry on back Jake. I need you."

"Kat?" A voice in the darkness. She shifted; her back

ached. Again, "Kat?" softly spoken, familiar. She looked about. Jake was kneeling beside her in the darkness.

"Hi, sleepy." He put his hand on her upper arm; it was warm. "You slept the whole evening. How are you now?"

She sat up, stretched her back. "Ugh, this is a lovely couch but awful to sleep on." Then it came back to her. Her eyes teared up, glistening in the dim street lights from the window. She threw her arms around Jake and sobbed into his shoulder, "My flat... Mrs Wilkins..."

"I know," he answered, "I saw it all this morning. It was horrible."

"What am I going to do?" she moaned.

Jake pulled back, held her softly by her shoulders, "Let me help you," his eyes locked to hers in the gloom, "stay here. You can stay as long as you need. We make a good team." he finished, slightly awkwardly.

Kat wiped her eyes messily on her sleeves and sniffed, "We do, don't we." She studied his face, "I like it here... with you."

"I think right now we both need each other," Jake said, "We should stick together... Just, you know, platonic." He looked down. Kat could tell he was blushing.

"No monkey business?" she smiled.

"No monkey business. You have my word."

"Then it's a deal." She leaned forwards and planted a little kiss on his forehead.

"I don't know about you, but I think I need a drink." he declared.

"Too bloody right." Kat agreed, getting to her feet and testing her knee. It was fine now, if a little stiff from the couch.

Jake busied himself switching on some lamps, then fetched a pair of chunky tumblers clinking with ice from the kitchen.

"Brandy, for shock they say don't they?" He opened up a cabinet and produced an impressive looking bottle "Croziet 1928 okay for you?" he asked with a put-on posh accent.

"Well, if that's all you have, okay" Kat chuckled.

He poured a generous slug of deep amber cognac and offered his glass for a toast.

"No monkey business!" He clinked his glass against hers, watching as she took a sip.

"Mmmm. Tastes like raisins." She raised her glass and Jake took a gulp. "I didn't know you were a connoisseur."

"Pfft, hardly. I just Googled 'expensive brandy' and bought one that looked fancy." He admitted.

"Blimey, how much did it cost?" She took a sniff.

"About the same as that 100 inch TV!"

Kat spluttered, "Shit! You're crazy! How can you blow that much on a bottle of booze?"

"Honestly, I've done okay with *Princess Sparkles*. I just wanted to see if there was anything to overpriced bottles." He took another sip.

"But isn't it a waste? Honestly, it's totally up to you what you do with your money – God knows, you've earned it."

"The *big* money's all looked after, I won't go mad and blow it all. But it's also a waste to just stick it all in a hole to rot, don't you think?"

Kat nodded, "You're right, I guess."

"Besides, it's always just me here on my own. I don't really have anyone to share it with." The mood turned sombre, "This brandy has been waiting nearly a hundred years to he shared."

Kat smiled and shuffled a little closer on the couch.

"I think it would be happy that it was you," he said quietly.

"Aww, that's sweet Jake," Kat snuggled against him.

CHAPTER 9

Thursday 18-March 2021.

  Moonrise: 08:10. Set: 23:47. (23.5%)
  Sunset: 18:15.

THE APARTMENT WAS virtually silent. Kat was curled up on the couch, Jake curled behind her legs, chin resting on the back of her knees.

She idly stroked his ear as she went over and over her deepest thoughts. Most people would have laid there telling their dog what was on their mind – she didn't really have any reason to *hide* anything from Jake...

Her mind was going in circles. She felt guilty about what was effectively a free-ride, staying here rent free. Jake wouldn't hear of her paying, he insisted that he had plenty of money.

She didn't want to take advantage, but she'd seen some of the royalty statements that Jerome had prepared – honestly, it was crazy money, EVERY month!

She thought about Jake; she ran her hand along his back – his fur so soft and golden, irresistible... Was he snoring now? He was such a nice guy, but naïve, a loner – like herself, she supposed. And smart. It seemed that anything he drew turned to gold. That stupid bloody unicorn. Shit, they were selling his comics and lunchboxes in Japan for God's sake. "Like bringing coals to Newcastle" her dad would have said... If he were still around. I guess they had something else in common since her mum died last year.

Both only children, parents gone; alone in the world and clinging to each other like pieces of driftwood in a stormy ocean.

So, what *was* their relationship? Was it just convenience? Was she just the dog-sitter, was he just her landlord? Flatmates, best friends *without* benefits?

Kat took a mental step back. Technically, she could just as easily have crashed with one of her girlfriends, but she felt more at ease here with Jake, with him. Calm, controlled. *Werewolf.*

It really had only been a few days, so how on Earth had this become normal? *"Love is the suspension of disgust"*... who had said that? She wracked her brain, watching the wind batter a long perished plant in a huge black pot out on the terrace.

The door intercom chimed. This time, Kat knew who it would be. Jake was till sleeping on the couch when she returned from the font door clutching a smallish cardboard pouch. She smiled at the gently snoring dog and quietly set the package on the coffee table.

It was nearly midnight when Jake transformed. His recovery was so much faster now, no more than if he'd just spent a half hour on a running machine.

Freshly showered and changed, he joined Kat for a bowl of instant noodles, a welcome midnight snack for them both.

"No, hold the first one like a pencil," He instructed Kat as she picked her chopstick off the floor. They were both sitting cross-legged on the rug in front of the coffee table. Jake had hungrily and expertly demolished half his noodles again before Kat had made much progress. But she insisted that he teach her how to use sticks this time – even if she starved to death in the process.

"Yes, that's it. So this one doesn't move, but don't grip it that tightly, you'll get a cramp." He watched Kat carefully lift a few strands of noodles out of the bowl of soup, slowly bringing her lips closer. The noodles slipped back into the bowl and the hot soup splashed onto Jake's arm.

He yelped and snatched his arm away, "Fuck! Kat, you FUCKWIT!" He slapped the bowl off the table. It careened across the floor spinning into the wall and shattered.

Kat leapt backwards across the side of the couch, stumbled and fell onto her back. Her eyes were wide with terror darting from Jake and towards the door. Jake jumped up, clutching his arm and roared.

"Jake! What–" she cried. It felt like a nightmare, what was happening to Jake? She scrambled to her feet, stifling a sob and fled, slamming the apartment door behind her.

Alone, Jake dropped to his knees, dazed. His arm was burned, it hurt... where was Kat? What had just happened? He looked around, saw the broken shards, food stuck to the wall.

"What have I *done*?" he breathed. "Kat?" he ventured. He got up and started towards the bedroom, the front door was ajar where it had bounced back open. He crept towards the door, listening carefully, he called in a low voice "Kat? Are you there?" Nothing.

Barefoot, he padded down the corridor towards the lift. It was parked at his level; it sometimes did that when it hadn't been used for a while.

He remembered the tale they'd told the police – had she gone up on the roof? He pushed the door open and made his way up the double flight of concrete steps, they were cold.

At the top, he paused, then slowly pushed the door open; the spring-loaded fire hinge was stiff.

Up on the rooftop garden it was dark, save for a few pools of light from decorative lamps. This late there was virtually no traffic noise from the street below. The door closed behind him, making him jump. The sound of the breeze was beginning to spook him, the vastness of the open sky, the depths to the street below. He wanted to crouch for fear of falling, his head span for a moment, pulse racing.

Jake's eyes were adjusting to the dark now, there was nobody to be seen. Past a nearby seating area, there was a trellis and another set of tables and chairs beyond, hidden from view.

"Kat, it's me, Jake," he whispered, "where are you?" A sound. Just the slightest of movements gave her away.

"Stay away." Her voice was trembling, tiny in the darkness.

Jake rounded the wooden lattice. Here and there topiary bushes in angular zinc planters cast shapes and shadows from the knee-height lights. There, under a bulky wooden table Kat was crouching. She backed up a little as Jake approached. "The Wolf, Jake. It's coming."

Jake lowered himself to the ground to be at the same

level, but he kept his distance. Something really had Kat spooked. "I don't understand. What wolf, what happened just now?"

"You don't remember?" She was just a shadow under the table.

"Last thing, I remember we were eating, next... you were gone, the smashed bowl."

"Marcus mentioned The Wolf in one of his emails; he said it could come in time. But he wouldn't tell me over the internet; that's why he insisted we go see him, and soon."

Jake let out a juddering sigh. This Marcus guy, he really did seem to have some kind of clue.

"Do you think we ought to see him sooner? You think we're– no, *you're* in danger?"

"Yes." Kat moved forwards, her face appearing out of the shadows, ghostly pale. "I think we should go tomorrow night." She crawled out and wrapped her arms around him, "And no, I don't think you'd ever hurt me." She looked at him, the fear in her voice melting away, "I know you care, Jake. I know that there's almost nothing that would bring you up here on the roof." She laid her head on his shoulder, "You came up here for me."

They sat, holding each other in silence while the quiet sounds of the night flowed around them. In the distance, a fox barked, plaintive, other-worldly.

Despite the warmth of Jake's body, Kat started to shiver.

"Come on, let's get inside." Jake suggested standing and offering a hand to Kat to help her up. A simple gesture, but it touched her heart.

"I just remembered." Kat said softly as they made their way down the stairs. She took him by the hand and hurried him back to the apartment.

"Stay there, *stay*," she said playfully, and ran to the bedroom, returning a moment later.

Jake looked at her quizzically as she handed him the package from earlier.

"I bought you a present." she said, smiling.

"Wow, really?" Jake brightened, "You don't need to." But he still ripped the cardboard open excitedly.

He laughed, and threw his arms around her, hugging her tightly then held up his new, blue collar, XL size WITH DINOSAURS!

"You've outgrown your old puppy collar, figured you needed a new one." Kat chuckled.

"I guess, in any other situation this would be regarded as pretty kinky," he said, clipping the collar on. He stood and struck a pose. "What do you think?"

"Oh yes suits you just fine!" she laughed. "Let's give it a test-drive at the park tomorrow. Anyhow, you're going to need to be properly dressed when we go visit Marcus."

"Oh, yes. That." He sat down, on the couch still wearing his collar.

"You nervous?"

"Yep. Though I can't think whether I'm more worried about going out or what we might find out."

"You'll be fine." She reminded him.

"Hope so." He straightened, "Right. Look I know we've had a freaky evening, but I've got to get that story outline sorted out for Jerome..." He stopped, thinking about something, fingering the collar "Hey,

I reckon Kids would go mad for *Princess Sparkles* pet collars! I'll email Jerome later."

Kat rolled her eyes as he sat at his drawing desk and flicked on the lamp. It was a stupid idea, but she knew it would make him a mint.

While Jake sketched, Kat padded to the bedroom to fetch her book. After sleeping earlier, she was wide awake – reading usually relaxed her. As she rummaged in her bag, the letters she brought back from her flat dropped out. Amongst them was the one from her landlord, the one that old Mr Rudd said she really ought to read. She stared at it nervously then tucked it into her book and went back to join Jake.

"How's it going?" she asked, resting her hands on his shoulders.

"Good, good. You know, one advantage to dog-time is that I get a lot of time to really *think*. Dogs don't really have a lot on their minds most of the time."

Kat snorted and tousled his hair.

"So, I think I've figured out a really neat finale."

"Finale? You're ENDING Rising Flesh?" Again, Kat was aghast, "I thought you'd decided to save things?"

"No, I need Michelle for the end." He explained, "Anyhow, I want to move on. It's been defining me for the last five years, holding me back. I feel that now's the time to do that. I haven't dared before."

Kat sighed, "So, quit while you're ahead?"

Jake nodded.

"Okay, what happens then?"

"Give me a couple of days." he said, tapping his pencil against his teeth, "It needs to be right. It's simple, but it'll blow you away. And no chance of a reprise later on."

"Gah! You and your infuriating cliff-hangers." She stomped off to the couch with her book, grinning.

Despite the shock earlier, she felt that things were going to be okay.

CHAPTER 10

Friday 19-March 2021.

  Moonrise: 08:32. Set: 0:55. (32.2%)
  Sunset: 18:16.

"Jake, stop pacing. Come and sit for a minute." Kat patted the couch next to her. She had to admit to herself that she was also nervous about meeting Marcus, but it wouldn't help Jake's anxiety to show it.

He jumped up and laid his chin on her thigh.

"Taxi should be here in a couple of minutes. Just a short ride, don't worry." Kat checked her phone again. No new messages from Marcus. He'd texted his location earlier that evening. Her phone buzzed; a notification – from the taxi company. It was three minutes away.

"Okay, time to go." She announced cheerfully Jake's ears pricked up and he jumped down panting excitedly. "Good to see that the dog part of you is okay with going out," she chuckled, clipping his lead on. She slung a rucksack over her shoulder and they headed out.

Just after the lift had begun to descend, it stopped – one floor down. The door opened revealing *Poirot*, carrying his little dog. Immediately, it began yapping at Jake. It was more one long joined up screech than a series of barks. Kat winced at the noise as the doors closed. The man was dressed in some kind of smoking jacket, and was he in Pyjamas? Kat stared ahead trying to ignore the pair – he made no attempt to acknowledge Jake and Kat, nor did he try to stop Foufou barking.

Jake looked up at the little dog, emitted one thunderous bark that shook the lift car. Foufou was immediately silenced and tried to burrow deeper into her master's arms.

As for *Poirot*, his look of disapproval ratcheted up several levels. His little moustache trembled with indignation as his eyes bored holes into the lift door.

Kat stifled a laugh as Jake sat, panting.

The lift came to a gentle rest and the doors opened. Kat and Jake stepped out, but *Poirot* and his little dog remained. She looked back, wondering why they weren't getting out. As the doors closed again, Kat noticed a puddle on the floor.

"That's quite a big puddle for such a small dog, don't you think?" she said. Jake panted and huffed.

The taxi app chimed at the exact moment that a cab stopped on the road outside the lobby. Jake wagged his tail and eagerly followed Kat into the back. The dog friendly cab had a large interior like the big black ones she sometimes took when she needed to go to London. No need for the owner to worry about dog hair or worse on the seats. There was plenty of space for luggage, she noted as the cab pulled away.

Jake lifted his nose and sniffed at the windows as they made their way through unfamiliar streets and onto the dual carriageway that led to the next town. Eventually, that road would take them, to coast. *That* would be quite an adventure to take Jake on some day.

"Jake, you want to go see the sea some day?" she

said quietly. The road was dark outside and he'd lost interest in that for now. His chin was resting on the bag but he lifted his head up and made a little nod to Kat before flopping down again.

The driver ignored her, though he probably couldn't hear her talking with her dog through the thick plastic divider.

It wasn't long until they reached the junction, and the cab swung gently off to the left into orange pools of light that swept across Kat's face.

They passed a gigantic Tesco superstore on their left, the car park populated by a handful of cars taking advantage of the 24 hour opening. *Looks like a good place to shop*, she though to herself, *wonder if there's a bus*. She snorted, laughing at herself, *Oh, God am I getting old? Checking out supermarkets.*

The cab turned into what looked like the older part of the town, away from the pedestrianised streets with their copy and paste rows of shops.

A few of the shops here had closed down, though the road didn't look shabby or run-down.

The cab slowed and stopped. Kat's phone lit up, the app begging a rating for the driver. She tapped 5 stars because... well why not. The driver turned around and spoke for the first time.

"Cheers Luv." He had a middle-eastern look about him, little goatee and a kind face. "Have a good evening." No trace of an accent though.

They jumped out into the empty street and the taxi – an electric one, she noted, slid quietly away.

Kat looked up at the sign above the shop, 'Crystal Energy' was painted in light coloured ornate letters on a dark, maybe blue background. The sodium lights made it hard to tell the true colour. No 72. was painted in slightly more formal script above the doorway itself. *Oh, that figures*, Kat recalled Marcus' username. She just assumed it was his year of birth as a lot of people added to their usernames online.

She peered through the glass of the shop window. It was almost completely dark inside. Behind the glass were an array of crystals, bulky salt lamps, mysteriously shaped glass apparatus which she assumed were used for smoking 'magical herbs'.

The usual hippy-shit. The shop inside didn't look that big, but it appeared to be packed with shelves and glass cabinets full of... who knew what.

There was a worn-looking bell push on the wooden door frame. She gave it a try, worrying that somehow she'd made some terrible mistake and there was nobody here.

Jake had taken an interest in the lamp post on the pavement behind them. She stepped back to indulge him. He peed against it, for longer than she thought possible.

"Wow, you needed that. Probably should have gone before we left." Jake huffed at her, then his ears pricked up and he looked towards the shop door.

A figure loomed behind the glass of the door, the lock clicked and rattled before the door slowly opened accompanied by the melodic *clonk* and *blong* of bamboo chimes attached to the ceiling above.

"You must be Kat," the man spoke in soft tones, "and no doubt this handsome fellow must be Jake." He opened the door and ushered them inside. He saw her glance at the 'no dogs' sticker on the glass of the door, "Perhaps, an exception in this case."

The man – he hadn't actually introduced himself yet – leaned outside and glanced down the street before closing and carefully locking the door.

"Okay, come to the back. We can talk in the treatment room."

They followed him through the shop where light was spilling through a gap in a pair of heavy velvet curtains. He held them open for Kat and Jake.

It wasn't a small room, it must have been pretty much the width of the shop, but it was stuffed full of mystic paraphernalia. Against one wall, a bed / chaise longe lurked under a mountain of tasselled pillows. Opposite that, a huge and ancient wing-backed chair dominated the room from behind a low, square table on which were neatly placed two decks of Tarot cards and a small ornate bottle.

Kat ducked under the chiffon swag hanging from the ceiling and took a seat on the edge of the bed. Jake slunk in behind her and sat, pressing against her leg. He glanced up at the slowly changing Christmas tree lights strung up with the gauzy material above.

"So. Kat, Jake, this is a rare pleasure." He lowered himself into the large chair, leaned forwards and addressed Jake directly "I've only met someone with your condition once before. Though I know of three others in the world living today."

Jake tilted his head, listening, "Now, I expect that you can understand a lot of what I'm saying right now Jake but, and I mean no offence to your canine spirit, I would prefer to discuss the more important aspects with you once you return to your human form."

Jake nodded slowly.

"Do you think there's a cure?" Kat piped up, "Perhaps something to do with these crystals." She waved her hand at the rows and rows of gems, some mounted into necklaces, hanging on the walls, others stacked in an array of little boxes on shelves.

Marcus laughed and stroked his neatly trimmed goatee. "These? No, I'm afraid not. These are just for the punters." his *educated* accent slipped for a moment – East London perhaps?

"Huh?" Kat was taken aback, "I thought you were genuine!"

"Oh, dear girl," back with the smooth drawl, "I can assure you, I am. This," he waved dismissively at the crystals, the bottles of oil with mysterious objects floating in them, "It's just a front. It distracts the inquisitive from my true work – and of course we do need funds to do what we do."

"We? There's others?"

"Indeed, we keep watch. We are always on the lookout for true supernatural events and we strive to protect them. Allow me to explain more about that later, it will be important for yourself and the young man here." He glanced at his watch, "Ah, I do believe he will be returning to us very shortly." Jake looked up at Kat, alarmed, whined.

"Oh, crap, yes." Kat reached for the rucksack and pulled out the big bathrobe. She draped it over Jake just as he yelped.

In the dim light of Marcus' treatment room the golden mist seemed even more beautiful. It twinkled in places where it caught the light from candles that Kat hadn't noticed before.

Knots and tendrils of gold flowed silently around Jake, finding their way into the robe through the sleeves, underneath, behind the collar.

Marcus sat motionless, taking it all in, smiling serenely, he lowered his head and closed his eyes as if in prayer as the final blast of mist rushed inwards.

Jake coughed experimentally and pulled the robe around himself. "Quite something, isn't it. Hi." he said to Marcus.

"Yes, quite something," he echoed. "It never gets old – and thank you so much for permitting me to witness this most sacred event."

"S'okay," Jake replied. "Can I go change – into some clothes, that is? It's a bit cold."

"Of course." Marcus indicated another set of curtains, "That should suffice."

Jake took the rucksack, grinning at Kat, who silently mouthed "Hi" back at him.

The space behind the curtains wasn't quite what Jake had expected. Rather than some inner sanctum, it was just a small kitchenette. He pulled the light cord that dangled to one side and the fluorescent tube above him reluctantly blinked on.

Nothing mysterious here; Kettle, microwave, a small stack of loo rolls on the floor under the sink.

He quickly pulled on some warm jogging pants and a hoodie, switched off the light and returned.

Kat slid over to let Jake sit next to her, there seemed to be an awkward silence in the room.

"So, I suppose you're wondering about your...

Condition?" Marcus started. They both nodded eagerly.

"There are two types. Yours, you might be interested is the rarest. 'Spontaneously Expressed Lycanthropy' is the generally agreed term. About one in four hundred Lycanthropes – werewolves, if you like – develop the condition for no discernible reason."

"And the rest?" Kat made a mock biting expression. Jake sniggered.

"Indeed. As the movies and books rightly suggest, it can be spread through bites – though," and he raised a finger to emphasise the coming point, "infection is very rare. You don't really need to worry too much about infection from bites, saliva… or other bodily fluids."

Jake grinned, blushing, Kat sighed in relief remembering the accident when Jake was a tiny puppy.

"How can you be sure though?" Jake asked.

"A good question. In recent years, we – and by *we*, I refer to a sizeable worldwide organisation, have moved from mysticism to science. The study of certain supernatural phenomena is quite a serious business."

"Can this *science* explain how I got this?" Jake asked.

"It's not entirely clear, but the best theory to date is that you have somehow encountered a splinter of animal life-energy."

"What, like a part of its soul?" asked Kat.

"Not exactly, it's more like the basic fundamental life-force. A part of what defines the essence of life – that *magical spark*."

"Midichlorians." Jake muttered under his breath.

Kat ignored him and pushed on.

"So why haven't we heard of this then? Why isn't it all in the public domain?"

"Simple. There are those that might seek to abuse such powers. We feed the media with superstition, cranks, fake videos and stories to keep these things in the realm of the incredible.

"You must know that we want NOTHING from you at all. We only seek to protect you, to stop you ending up on a table in some government laboratory."

Jake flinched at the thought. Kat held his hand and squeezed.

"There are members of our organisation that have been granted various supernatural 'gifts' – some see it as a curse. What we do is also for self-protection."

"You talked about 'The Wolf' the other day, but you wouldn't go into detail." Kat asked.

Marcus sat back, face grim. "Ah yes. The Wolf. Now here's where the folk tales and myths are born." He ran a hand down his goatee, smoothing it, "In most cases, lycanthropes lead a peaceful life between species and very often in control of the change–"

"Control? How?" Jake interrupted, excited. He looked at Kat, this was what they'd both hoped to hear.

"Let me come to that." Marcus said, holding his hand up, "As I said, most can control their changes, but sometimes there's a dark force that lurks behind. This can grow and take control if not kept in check."

"Like in the horror stories?" Kat asked. "That's all real?"

"Dramatised, but in essence yes." He leaned forwards, deadly serious. "If The Wolf is allowed to take control, then you could be lost to it – forever."

Kat was almost expecting a flash of lightning, but the only sound was the fridge motor starting up behind the curtain.

"Be on your guard for changes." He was looking at Jake now, "Mood swings, sudden anger, rage."

"It happened." Jake admitted quietly, "I lashed out at Kat yesterday. It was like I blacked out."

Marcus drew a long slow breath, "Okay. Well, we've caught it early, there's no need to panic. There are two things you can do to keep it in check. The first, you will like, the second... well, at first you may be repulsed."

"Okay, let's get the bad stuff out of the way." Jake said.

"For sure. Well, let me give this to you as simply as I can." He paused, composed himself, "The only guaranteed way to keep The Wolf suppressed is to kill."

Kat Gasped, "No. That can't be true!"

"Fresh blood is the only thing that will satisfy it."

"What, like a vampire?" asked Jake.

Marcus shot him a withering look, "There's no such thing as vampires, they're just made up.

"But the good news is that once you have made your kill, you WILL be free for seven years."

"I can't murder!" Jake rasped, "I'd rather die."

"No, no. You don't have to take a human life. A sheep, a deer, any reasonably large animal will work. It's okay, we've been covering this up for hundreds of years – unexplained mauling of livestock, blame it on a wolf from the forest, nowadays a rogue dog... Aliens even. People are easy to fool if you can just give them a scapegoat to point the finger at."

"I don't even think I can do that," Jake moaned. "Can't I just eat a raw steak or something?"

"No. There's a difference, you must kill. It's thought that freshly killed flesh still contains life-force, and that's what restores the balance. Butchered meat is just dead matter." He looked Jake in the eye, smiled faintly, "Don't worry, when the time comes, you'll do it. But you'll need to exercise control over your transformations first, so that you can choose your prey wisely."

Jake sighed, "Okay, if you say so. So what's the other part?"

Marcus clasped his hands together, "Now. This is honestly the best part; it can put you back in control of your life. What if I were to tell you that you could control the shape of your animal form?"

Jake sputtered "Seriously? Like I can change into different animals?"

"No," Marcus laughed, "That's not possible, though there was one a case of someone being infected with two energies at once – quite odd. No, you will always naturally transform to the essential form of the animal who's essence you possess – not the actual animal, as I suggested, just the nature of it. But if you were to exert control during the transformation itself, then you can retain most of your natural form."

"That's fantastic," Kat said, "Jake, you can live a normal life!"

"Well, it's almost unheard of to be able to resist the animal form entirely, but you should be able to keep your general body shape – arms, legs, fingers. You should be able to function more or less normally. But there will still be some features; usually it's hair, facial features. For some reason most people find it very hard to deal with tails."

"So, how's it done?" Jake asked.

"Simple. When you feel the transformation happening, you only need to focus on your own body shape. Think hard about your own being, who you are, your form. It does take a little effort, and you won't get it right first time."

"Really, that's all there is to it?" Jake was shaking, a tear forming in his eye. "I had no idea. I really thought I was going to have to live half my life as a dog."

Kat put her arm around him and pulled him close, "This is really the best news."

"Any other advice?" asked Jake cheerfully.

"Well, avoid silver. It's toxic to you now. Skin contact might give you a rash... Oh, and don't eat chocolate when in dog form!" he chuckled.

He clapped his hands together with a kind of finality, it seemed the session was going to be over, "I won't keep you good people any longer Besides, it's late and I have snake oil and charms to sell in the morning."

Kat ordered a cab, it looked like the same guy was still in the area and would only be a couple of minutes.

Marcus led them through the shop and out to the door. "Remember, if you ever need any help or advice just get in touch. Other than that, we'll just keep out of your hair and let you live your life. Good luck – to you both."

On cue, the taxi slid to a stop next to them.

"Hello again Miss," the taxi driver said through the little speaker, "where's your dog?"

"Oh, um, with a friend. He's dog sitting while we go away for a couple of days." Kat fumbled. Jake grinned in the waves of orange streetlights.

"Can you stop here?" Jake called as they approached the big park entranceway.

"What's up?" Kat whispered.

"I think I fancy a walk" Jake said, his eyes full of energy.

"This late, at night. Are you sure?"

"I've never been more sure." The cab stopped and Jake pulled her out by her arm. She was just about able to grab the rucksack as she tumbled out giggling. She caught the driver smiling and shaking his head as Jake whisked her through the gateway into the park.

"Let's go to the bridge." He sniffed deeply, the air was crisp and cold, "We can look at the stars."

Kat giggled, "This is crazy – but I love it." She linked her arm with his and they marched through the empty park beneath the ornate lamps.

There were a couple of benches in the middle of the wide footbridge, Kat snuggled into the warmth of Jake's hoodie as he lent back staring at the diamond studded sky.

"I don't even know if I can remember when I last looked at the stars," he said softly. "Even last night, I felt like I would drown out in the open on the roof."

"So, what changed?"

"I don't know, with each transformation I'm changing a little. Something more – free and natural is seeping into me, or maybe those broken, twisted parts are simply being left behind each time, little by little."

"Are you sure it's not The Wolf, like Marcus said?" Kat was worried.

"Perhaps. I mean – maybe it's driving out my old demons, purging me of the human frailties that have held me back."

"I hope so, but we need to be careful. I can't go through what happened last night again."

Jake put his arm around her and pulled her tighter, "I promise that'll never happen again. I'll go get some fresh meat if I have to. We ought to figure out what to do when the time comes."

She looked up at him, "We'll figure it out," then, "Are you going to try to control the transformation tomorrow?"

He stroked her hair, "Absolutely." His phone chimed. It was his sky app. Kat sat bolt upright.

"What? You're not due until tomorrow morning!"

"It's okay," he soothed, "I also set it for the ISS."

And just as predicted, a bright white jewel sailed slowly and silently across the sky. They sat together in the cold night air until it vanished over the horizon.

CHAPTER 11

Saturday 20-March 2021.

  Moonrise: 09:00. Set: 02:00. (41.6%)
  Sunset: 18:18.

KAT WOKE BEFORE her alarm. Jake's transition was at 9am on the dot today. A surge of anxiety bubbled in her stomach. Today was the day that could change everything. Today, Jake was going to try to control his transformation.

She looked over at Jake – still sleeping peacefully. They had about an hour, she should wake him but they hadn't got back to the apartment until, what, 2:30am?

They had sat under the stars, alone in the park talking about everything they had learned from Marcus that night. It was a lot to take in, if the world was already turned on its head, the revelation that there was a global secret society had blown what was left of their minds.

Kat watched Jake a little longer. So peaceful. She remembered how they had staggered back into the apartment like a couple returning home drunk from a big night out. Exhausted, they just fell into bed and were both fast asleep before they even knew it. The pillow ritual forgotten, they lay redundant on the floor – *perhaps*, thought Kat *we don't need these any more.*

The   bond   between   them   had   strengthened

immeasurably these last two days. They had faced near catastrophe, she had seen Jake's caring side. Willing to face his fears up on the roof for her.

Had they finally drifted inescapably towards each other? Was it inevitable? Kat wasn't sure. They would have just carried on as they had done for years, polite, business-like, just workmates. This thing had torn down all those walls, thrown them together. There may not have been a future for them in the old world. But in this new, strange world... she realised that the possibilities were exciting. Should she just give in to what was happening and let it carry her along? In a sense, she didn't have a great many options, but life here with Jake was good. She had kept returning to that thought, she knew it.

Okay, she would go with her gut, go with what felt right. Jake was so shy, but the casual affection last night seemed so natural.

Jake stirred. Kat stroked his hair, smiling. He hadn't shaved for a couple of days – it didn't really make for much of a rugged look. Some guys – well, a bit of stubble lent macho appeal – Jake, well, not with his skinny bod. She laughed to herself, he'd forgotten his t-shirt. Hopefully, he had remembered his shorts. The poor guy was so self-conscious. Should she check?

Yes, better do, she peeked under the covers – oops! Good morning, to you too mister!

Time to save the day before Jake woke.

Quietly, Kat leaned over the edge of the bed, grabbed a couple of pillows and slid them under the duvet along his body. They were so beat last night that he'd just think they'd put them there out of routine. There!

Modestly protected!

She looked at her phone. 8:03. *We'd better get this day going.*

"Jake." she called softy, stroking his hair again. "Time to wake up."

He stirred, turned from his back and hugged the pillows between them. *Phew – good call!* His eyes opened slowly, facing her, focused. A smile spread slowly across his face as he came to.

"Oh... Hey," he rasped. "morning." his face froze, patted the pillows then relaxed.

"Don't worry–" Kat reassured him.

"No monkey business." He finished for her. They laughed together.

"I'll pop to the loo while you –"

He nodded bashfully. *So shy*, she thought to herself again in in the bathroom. *Cute.*

Jake sat on the edge of the couch, robe tied firmly around himself. He'd drunk a double shot in his coffee already. They'd both needed a bit of a boost.

"One minute to go." Kat announced. Jake stiffened. "Remember, when it comes on think 'Jake' thoughts. Think about yourself, how you look, who you are."

He nodded, gulped. His throat was dry but it was too late to do anything about that now. The tell-tale pressure was building in his head.

Okay, this was it. His vision blurred, the itching in his skin. *Thoughts... Not... No, think Jake. I am Jake, I am... I...* He pictured himself in the mirror, his face... *Two arms, legs... Skinny legs, unremarkable... Small... She said It's small. No, who cares, I am Jake, I am me.*

"I am Jake." He rasped faintly. It was over. He was curled up on the floor, in or under the robe. He was tired.

Jake gathered himself and got slowly to his feet. Had it worked? Two legs. He was standing upright.

Something under the robe moved and stood up. Kat gasped. A laugh burst unbidden from her mouth, stifled immediately.

"Well, It's a start, I guess." she said uncertainly.

Between the couch and the table, a figure, half wrapped in the bath robe stood all of three feet tall. Thin, pink with fine, golden tufts of hair sprouting patchily over his body.

"Oh Fuck..." Jake patted himself all over, looking from one arm to the other, held his left leg up and wriggled his surprisingly normal toes.

Kat choked back a laugh – not fair, but... "Shit, Jake, you look like Dobby and Golem had a baby!" She lowered herself to her knees to get to eye-level. "Come here," she soothed.

Jake tottered over and let Kat hold him tightly.

She let go and he adjusted his robe the best he could.

"Hands," he said looking at his fingers. He opened and closed them experimentally. "Bloody brilliant!" he beamed, "Okay, this isn't right but honestly, first try – not terrible." His voice was somewhat squeaky and the comedy value of that certainly wasn't lost on Kat.

"What do you think went wrong then?" she asked.

"I think I just lost concentration." he mused, "Once the change starts, I think the mind begins to change first. I can sort of feel my mind..." he hunted for the word, "Simplifying? I must have let it slip too far, it was really hard to think." He smiled, "Hands though! This is a gamechanger. Okay, I look like a freak but I can work, I can DO stuff."

Kat saw it from his perspective now, "Oh my God, you're right!" Kat thrilled, "You're going to be okay."

"If I can improve on this," he held his arms out to his sides and turned slowly around, "then that's gonna be good for you too. I mean, you can get back to work."

Kat nodded, though she still felt the hot breath of the elephant in the room breathing down her neck. If Jake could now live independently, then what would that mean for her? Would he send her on her way? The thought made her heart sink.

"What's wrong?" Jake asked, lifting himself up on to the couch with a grunt.

Should she bring it up? She was torn. Was Jake's offer to let her stay really just a matter of convenience, or... and here she was again circling back to the question about how she truly felt about Jake. *Come on Kat, admit it You DO really like him.*

"Um, nothing." she muttered. Come on, let's get some breakfast. *Shit, Kat, when are you going to face up to it?*

Jake was at his desk again, furiously scratching away with a pencil. He had had to raise the draughtsman's chair up to the maximum height and add a cushion.

Kat had a little work to do plus an email for Jerome to write, they'd agreed to break the news tomorrow morning.

"Look, I think I can try for a 'normal' day today." Jake had said earlier holding a pencil. "If I can get the outline for the end of TRF together, then we can present it to Jerome on Monday morning, before I change."

Kat pulled a dubious expression, "Okay, he's still going to lose his mind, but I'll set up a meeting first thing on Monday. What time are you changing on Monday?"

Jake picked up his phone, snorted "Ugh, fingerprint recognition doesn't work." He stabbed his password at the screen, "Ten twenty-four."

"Okay, that'll be enough time. We can piggyback that onto the Monday production meeting – everyone should be there. I'll set it for Nine thirty, half an hour for you to talk, assume a few minutes overrun, should be good."

"Great." said Jake, fiddling with his chair. There was a sucking sound and the chair rose up slowly on its piston. "You want to hear what I've got planned?" He spun the chair around, miscalculated and sailed back round to face the window.

Kat chucked as he cranked himself back round again, "No, save it for the meeting. I really don't think I'd be able to hold it in until then." Her eyes started to brim with tears, "This is really the end of an era Jake." She wiped her eyes with the back of her hand, "Sheesh," she examined the wetness, "Look at me; crying over a comic book. There's going to be a lot of disappointed fans."

"Maybe," Jake said, "But something that I've learned this last few days is that change comes, and you have to deal with it." His voice, as best it could, grew serious, "I could have drawn that *damn comic* for years and years, going nowhere, losing characters, gaining new ones, but ultimately just plodding on and on. No conclusion..." He sighed, "I don't know, it just feels like that's how my life had been. I was just plodding on, doing what I knew, avoiding change and growth, being shut in and not facing up to my anxieties."

Kat was rapt, Jake had stopped to breathe.

"Go on." She urged softly.

"I want to break free of that. I want to live my life. Kat, all this has shown me what I *really* want–" He stopped, looked at his hands for a long second. "I know that I'm going to be able to look after myself now. I know that I asked if you'd stay here to help me. But I think that needs to change, I think we both knew that was going to happen."

Kat felt a burn of fear wash outwards from her stomach, her eyes started to moisten again, what was he trying to say?

"Kat... Will you stay here? Will you stay with me," his words were clumsy, he'd never been here before, "like, you know properly *move in*? Sorry, do you think I'm being–" he didn't get to finish his sentence; Kat had scooped him up off the stool like a toddler and hugged him.

"Oh, Jake of *course* I will." she swung him round, legs flailing. The tears were rolling down her cheeks now, washing away the anxious drops that had been forming a few seconds earlier. Brave, brave Jake – he must have been fighting with this for days, plucking up the courage.

She realised that he was dangling rather undignified. She carefully put him down. He straightened his baggy t-shirt and cleared his throat.

"Good." he said, and returned to his work.

Kat sat on the couch. Her head was swimming, and not from spinning Jake around. 'Good' she laughed to herself, he's a funny sort of a guy. But she loved him. It hit her, like a warm tsunami – she *loved* him.

Sunday 21-March 2021.

Moonrise: 09:37. Set: 02:58. (51.6%)
Sunset: 18:20.

Sunday was a lazy day for Kat. With all that had happened in the last week, she finally had a chance to have a 'normal' day. Jake had attempted to control his transformation that morning, and the results were far better. He was able to keep his bathrobe on throughout and at the end of it he was only perhaps a couple of inches shorter. He'd kept a lot of his fur and it was smooth and even.

"That's actually, not a bad look for you," Kat had remarked, giving him a long hug then stroked his chest – she started to wonder if she actually got off on his silky fur. The tail, as Marcus had predicted remained and his face was still almost entirely doggy.

"I think you should just keep the dog face, it's really cute." She scratched him behind the ear and they collapsed with laughter when his leg involuntarily started to twitch.

The rest of the day, Kat binged TV in her pyjamas

while Jake worked on his drawings. Bliss!

The de-transformation wouldn't happen until just before 3am. With work on Monday, Kat really couldn't wait up for Jake to return to normal so she turned in around 11pm.

"I'm just checking these storyboards," Jake called after Kat, "I'll be with you in a bit."

Kat stopped and turned, smiling, "I don't know how you've kept going all day – you've hardly stopped working."

He looked up from the board, "Nor do I," he admitted, "I've had so much energy today, everything's just been so clear in my mind." He ran his hands through his golden, floppy ears, "Think I'm feeling it now though." He yawned, big white dog-teeth showing.

Kat woke in darkness. Jake had slipped into bed quietly, hoping not to wake her.

"Hey there," she said sleepily, "Did you get it all finished?"

"Yep, it's all packed up for you to take in tomorrow." He scratched, "Let me talk it through on video in the meeting before you hand over the art. I don't want Jerome to flip out."

Kat agreed with him and turned to face him. Her eyes adjusting to the dark.

"Sheesh," it's really hot with all this fur. He sat up and stripped off his t-shirt and flopped back down again on his back. "Better."

Kat reached a hand over and stroked his chest slowly.

"Jake?" she whispered, "can we take away the top

pillow? I could just fall asleep in that soft fur of yours." God, she wanted to be rid of the lot of them and to hell with the consequences. He was just SO heart-achingly soft and warm and snuggly – and because he showered every day and brushed his teeth, no doggy smell!

"I guess so," said Jake pulling the pillow out and lofting it over the bed onto the floor.

Kat snuggled closer and drifted off into the most peaceful sleep with her head buried into the velvety fur of Jake's chest.

Monday 22-March 2021.

Moonrise: 10:24. Set: 03:48. (61.7%)
Sunset: 18:21.

Today was a caramel latte with whipped cream kind of day. Kat put the half-finished cup – oh, it had to be a LARGE one – down on her desk and logged into her computer.

The meerkats had popped up as she breezed through the studio to her double-sized cubicle outside Jerome's office. Word had gotten out that Jerome was pissed about something again, so how come Kat was in such a good mood?

Mario was looking at her quizzically, from behind his big digital drawing board. He was hoping that maybe she would enlighten him. She just smiled back, collected some papers from her printer, grabbed her coffee and headed for Jerome's office.

A couple of minutes later, Kat and Jerome paraded

into the big meeting room followed by a couple of the other execs.

It was nothing unusual; each Monday the leads met for a production meeting but there was a sense of gravity today that everyone on the office floor could feel. You could hear a pin drop until the glass door closed, and the e-glass snapped opaque. Then the whispering and gossip began.

Inside the meeting room, everyone took their usual seats. Kat handed out printed agenda sheets and sat next to Jerome. On the big screen at the end of the room, the video conference software had started.

Akiko had already signed in from their small office in Japan. She didn't usually attend Monday meetings, but Jerome had convinced her to hang back after hours for an important announcement.

Just then, Jake signed in. A dog face appeared next to Akiko. Kat choked on her latte, then Jake's face appeared.

"Um, you've got a new profile picture, Jake?" Kat blurted.

"Yeah, cute huh?" He grinned into the webcam.

"Okay." Jerome's voice was a little unsteady. "I understand that Jake has an announcement to make about '*The Rising Flesh*', to be honest, the first I'd heard of it was this weekend." He raised a hand to the screen at the end of the room, "Okay then. Let's have it."

"Right then." Jake started. "I'll cut to the chase. I'm going to finish *Rising Flesh*. This next series will be the last one – ever." He paused for a moment while the grumbles settled and a quiet "Fuck You" from the finance director.

"I want to move on to other projects later this year. But most importantly, I don't want to let the series stagnate. I want to finish it, and I want to do that on a hopeful, upbeat note.

"I've plotted out the key beats for the series, and Kat's brought in the sketches if you want to look at them in detail afterwards.

"But, look. Here's how it's going to end – in a nutshell. We know that Michelle survives the cliff-hanger. But the old train carriage she ends up in was being scouted by the Loco group. They're still on the move in their train, and their technology and numbers have grown.

"They capture Michelle for use in their ongoing research to find an end to the Zombie plague.

"Word gets back to Sarah and the rest of the group. The main thrust of the series is then their journey to hunt down the train, infiltrate it and rescue her mother." Jake took a breath; he was one hundred percent in his element here. "And, so to the finale. The Locos are developing a serum that they hope will stop the Zombie virus. But, and you guessed it, the only way to know if it works for sure is to KILL the test subject and find out if they come back or not.

"Sarah battles her way to the lab carriage on the train and finds her mother. She's tied to a table, the scientists are subdued and she looks down on her. The SECOND injection has been given.

"Tearful exchange, blah blah, Michelle dies... and STAYS DEAD!" He mimics an explosion with his hands, "It's all over, there's hope for humanity after all."

It took a couple of seconds before anyone reacted. Kat slowly closed her jaw – THAT was the other reason why she loved him so much. The boy was a genius!

"Holy fucking shit on a stick." Jerome said slowly. "Well, that's going to end the series for sure, but I love it! Jake, I love you!" There were assorted mumbles of assent from around the table. Akiko quietly wiped a tear from her eye, hoping nobody would see. Jerome clocked it, he'd been watching her face throughout the entire monologue. He trusted her judgement, and if this had moved her, then he was one hundred percent behind it.

"Good, then." he resumed, "Any questions to Jake?"

Kat noticed the time, 10:20, she jumped, made a point of clearing her throat loudly and surreptitiously tapped her wrist with a finger with meaningful look to Jake. He got it... *Crap! Just four minutes to go.*

"Er, sorry guys, I've got to... go see a man about a dog, if you know what I mean. Catch you later guys. Oh, Kat. That *cake*, I'm baking later, I'm going to try a new recipe. I think you'll like it. See you when you get home." He winked and disappeared, to be replaced by his dog profile picture. That was always going to unnerve Kat, she knew it.

All eyes slowly turned to Kat.

Jerome gave a certain look to Bev, the marketing lead, "Told you." he said cattily.

By lunchtime, the marketing and advertising groups had broken away into their own little huddles, and reported in with outlines of how they were going to ride out the end of one of their big money-spinners.

Kat was still on a high; the studio was suddenly vibrant and alive. There was change in the air; it was exciting and dangerous – like her own life right now.

Her phone chimed. There was a text from Jake.

> [JAKE] Holy shit! I think I've cracked it this time. You've GOT to see this. Like, right now!
>
> [KAT] What have you done? What happened?
>
> [JAKE] I think you need to see for yourself.

Kat had to think. How could she find an excuse to go back home? Pulling a sickie wouldn't really cut it so soon after the last one. She smiled to herself – 'home', Jake's apartment really *was* home now. Stop. Think now, she tapped her pen against her teeth – ah, that's it!

"Jerome?" Kat popped her head into his office. He was typing furiously, but – and this made her do a double-take – he was actually smiling. She couldn't remember the last time she had seen him actually smiling.

"Yuh?" he replied, not slowing down.

"Jake needs some more stationary; pretty urgent. Okay if I go drop it off with him?"

"Yuh," drifted over his screen. Ha, that was easy.

The door lock beeped and Kat struggled inside, laden down with a large package of paper. Jake jumped off the couch and stood in the living room, tail wagging furiously under his bath-robe.

Kat caught sight of him, stopping her dead; the package slowly slipped out of her hands and fell to the floor.

"...the... Fuck?" she whispered.

Standing, proudly in the middle of the room, Jake six foot tall, broad shoulders, the most dog-handsome face grinning, showing strong, white teeth, his floppy, golden ears alert.

"What do you think?" It was Jake's voice, but deeper, richer – fucking *Hollywood* rich. Kat approached him slowly, her mouth slightly agape. She placed a hand on his chest where the robe was open at the top. She clenched her fingers, trembling, took a handful of his soft golden fur, released it and smoothed it down, feeling the muscle underneath. She looked up and met his eyes; perfect, hazel brown, his nose glistened. Graceful whiskers swept out to each side, swayed as he spoke.

"So, you like it?" he asked softly.

"Fuck it, yes." she growled, taking him by the hand and dragging him towards the bedroom. Her strength caught him off guard and off balance and they stumbled and tumbled into the bedroom, the door crashing open. Using the physical and hormonal strength that suddenly possessed her, she threw him onto the bed. Her breath was ragged now, her face flushed, oh God this was it, this was what she had needed SO badly.

Jake lay on the bed where he had landed an expression of half surprise, half fascination as Kat hurled her jacket across the room followed by, shoes, jeans... cursing as they refused to part company.

She bounded onto the bed next to Jake on her hands and knees in her underwear and shirt – no time, deal with that in a second.

"Jake... You're... You're..."

"Ripped! Yeah, who needs a stupid gym?" he laughed.

She leaned over and kissed him. It was a little strange, she wasn't sure about that but not to worry, this was happening whatever. His teeth were so white and...

"Oh, Jake what beautiful teeth you have." She stroked a velvety ear and pulled open the robe revealing that silky soft fur that had her *so* turned on. She ran her hands over his chest.

"Oh, Jake," she kissed him once on each nipple – just the two? She'd find out in a moment, "what strong muscles you have." He twitched as she ran her fingers down his chest towards his stomach, pulling the belt apart a little more. His fur was growing shorter the further down she went, becoming a fine golden down, lighter in colour.

"Oh, Jake what beautiful ABS you have," She was enjoying the word-play here because she knew full well where this was going. She felt him tense his stomach muscles for her as she laid a hot trembling palm there.

The robe's belt was tied a little tight, and she grunted with frustration while she struggled with the knot. She could hear the blood pounding in her ears, her insides clenching, the burn of adrenaline in her stomach. But eventually, she had it and tore the robe fully open and gasped hoarsely, "Oh JAKE! What a big–"

It took a few minutes for Kat to get her breath back. She lay exhausted, flushed, but... oh, so much better.

Beside her, Jake was panting a little, but of course in

his current form, he was in much better shape than her. Despite that his big tongue lolled out of the side of his mouth, a slightly stupid expression on his face.

"You look like the cat that's got the cream, Jake," she gasped, trying to slow her breathing. Jake snorted. "Oh. Yeah, I suppose that would be me then technically." She giggled and snuggled into his soft fur. "Sheesh, that was quite something." Jake still didn't say anything. He'd put his tongue away but the beatific expression still remained.

"I've got something to tell you," he murmured at last. "I didn't really want to say. It's a bit embarrassing."

"A secret?" Kate gasped, turning on her side, palm pressed against his muscular chest. She kissed it, she couldn't resist. "What could you *possibly* have to tell me after all this?"

"That was my – well, my first time." He admitted. Kat burst out laughing and fell back onto the bed.

"Oh Jake... sorry I didn't mean to laugh." She slapped his arm playfully, "Well, for a first time, I think you did pretty bloody good." She stretched luxuriously, Jake was still staring at the ceiling, grinning.

"Well, if you really want to know, this is my first time with a wolf-man." She suddenly fell quiet. It had struck her. "Crap, Jake!" She sat up suddenly, pulling the duvet around herself. "What have we done?" There was a look of panic building in her eyes now.

Jake sat up and turned to her, she looked at his impossibly perfect physique, at his dog-face, the big bushy tail curled around behind him. "What is it?" he asked.

"This... this is all wrong. I don't know what I was

thinking... Jake, you know I love you, I love you so much, but I've just made love with a *dog*." Her blood ran cold, "Oh, Jake this is so wrong."

He pulled her close, wrapping a strong arm around her, "No, Kat. It's me, it's Jake. You remember what Marcus was saying about the animal fragment. It's just the 'essence' of the animal. This is me, here, Jake."

Her eyes were brimming. A tear rolled down her cheek as she turned to him. "Do you think so? Are you *sure* about that?" she asked, voice trembling. Suddenly, she was small, fragile.

"I know it." He replied, voice deep and smooth – comforting. She was feeling vulnerable, confused, but resting her head on his shoulder slowly she began to feel like she was safe again. Protected by 'her man'. She never thought that she would feel like that, she had always been so independent, never relying on anyone. Now she knew that she needed someone in her life to... to literally lean on when things got too much.

They sat there, quietly holding each other for several minutes. Each lost in their own thoughts, not knowing that they were both thinking the same thing. That they had found the one that they needed in their life, that they could never let go of each other – never.

Kat sniffed and wiped her nose on the back of her hand; she smiled through wet eyes and let a long breath slide out of herself. The warmth had crept back into her heart again. She looked at Jake; his ears pricked up when he felt her hand stray absently.

"Jake! My God, you *beast*, how are you still–"

It was late into the afternoon when Kat declared with

absolute *certainty*, that this time enough was enough. "I can't…" she gasped, "I really can't any more. I think I'm going to die. Come on dog, off the bed." She turned and playfully pushed Jake off the bed with both feet. He vanished over the edge then popped up, naked. To her relief, the only thing sticking up now was his magnificent tail. He turned around and it waved gently in the air.

Kat watched in amusement as he struggled with a pair of fresh sweat pants. There was just no place for his tail. Exasperated, he dropped them to the floor and opened a drawer, pulled out a pair of boxer shorts. After a small amount of negotiation, he threw his arms in the air, "Ta-da!"

He had the shorts on backwards with his tail protruding from the opening that would normally go in front. "How's that?" he asked proudly.

"Perfectly decent." Kat giggled.

Slowly, carefully, Kat lifted a dangling mass of noodles into her mouth.

"You got it!" Jake applauded. The pair were sat on the rug leaning against the couch tucking in to chicken chow-mien from the takeaway across the street. Kat had on a large t-shirt, an older one that bore the stains from earlier, less successful attempts with her chopsticks.

Jake was still just in his improvised dog-shorts – Kat had refused to let him put on a shirt and cover up "that scrummy bod" as she'd put it.

Jake put down the pair of disposable wooden sticks; they clattered in the empty foil container. He rubbed the back of his head.

"You okay?" Kat asked, cheating a little and stabbing a piece of chicken with a stick, "Why the hang-dog look?" she elbowed him, cheerfully, "'cos you're one hung-dawg!" she laughed.

Jake didn't respond. He seemed lost in thought. Kat's face drew serious now.

"Really, what's up. You don't look good."

"Yeah. Sorry, I just kind of feel really tense all of a sudden."

"The Wolf?"

"Yuh, could be." He got up and stood at the window. It was getting dark, but at least this weekend the clocks would go forwards. Spring was coming, and with it lighter evenings. The darkness felt so oppressive. He remembered being up on the roof, the dark sky seemed to be pressing down on him–

"Jake." Kat put a hand on his shoulder and he flinched. "I think it's time. We should call Marcus."

"I have to kill, don't I?" he muttered, looking past his reflection in the window.

"Yes." Kat said sadly, "It's the only way to keep The Wolf in its place."

"You're right," he sighed turning to her and taking her hands, "I don't ever want to hurt you or scare you like that again."

He held her tightly, her head buried in the warmth of his body.

Marcus had suggested a video call as soon as Kat messaged him.

He appeared in the video call; behind him a

psychedelic throw hung on the wall and he was surrounded by an assortment of crystals, statues and strange bottles.

"Guys. Hi. Good to see you both again. And Jake, wow! Just look at you!" The pair looked at each other and smiled, "Look, I've only guided a handful of lycanthropes before, and never have they been able to control their transformations so quickly and... well, so elegantly."

Jake, snorted bashfully, "You should have seen the first try!"

"Takes a strong mind. You have a powerful energy – no," He waved his hand about, "not 'crystal vibration energy' bollocks, I mean life energy."

"Thanks," Jake said a little uncertainly, "So. It's about this wolf thing. I'm starting to feel really... agitated, tense, you know what I mean?"

"Yes. Those are the early signs. You did the right thing to call me." He looked into the little camera lens, serious, "You know what you have to do?"

"No. I really don't. I feel a little sick about it to be honest."

"Don't worry." He sat back, his wicker chair creaked alarmingly, "If we put you in the right situation, The Wolf will know what to do."

Kat took Jake's hand and squeezed it, her face lit pale by the laptop screen.

"There's a field, about a mile north of where you are," Marcus continued, "you can get there directly from the canal path." He paused a beat, "There are sheep. Lots of them."

Jake shivered a little.

"I know the place," Kat filled the silence. "I've been there before."

"Good." Marcus smiled, "Obviously, you can't go out tonight like this – marvellous though it is. You're going to have to go tomorrow, late. Jake, you should take on dog-form for this, just let the change happen naturally when if comes."

Jake nodded, still silent.

"Besides," Marcus looked directly into the camera again, "You're going to need four legs for the chase and those big canines for the finish."

Jake looked away and let out a long, slow breath.

"It's okay Jake," he said, "you can do it. Practically everyone manages it first time, the instincts take over," he smiled, "You've got Kat to help you, let her take you there. And, look, I can't tell you how happy I am to see you both together. For most, this is a solitary life, to have a mate–" he stopped, "Well. Look, you're both going to be fine."

CHAPTER 12

Tuesday 23-March 2021.

  Moonrise: 11:24. Set: 04:29. (71.6%)
  Sunrise: 06:00. Sunset: 18:23.

Morning light leaked coldly round the bedroom curtains, it hit Kat's eyes and seemed to suck the warmth from her. Today was going to be dreadful, but there was no way to avoid it. She looked at her phone. It was a little past nine. They should sleep more, it was going to be a late night tonight and the day was just going to drag on – best to just sleep. Sleep the morning away.

Kat opened her eyes, it was brighter now, a thin shaft of light painted a stripe across the floor from a crack in the curtains towards the bed.

She rolled over and put her arm around Jake, the pillows of course were history.

He had changed late in the night, again so gently that she didn't wake. He was still sleeping, turned towards the edge of the bed, he hadn't put on a shirt from earlier.

Kat ran her hand down his side feeling his warm, hairless skin – skinny, but no matter, this was *her* Jake, her love.

"Don't," he murmured.

"Hmm? Don't, what?" she kissed the back of his neck. He curled away from her a little.

"I. I look like crap, not like yesterday."

Kat put her arm around him and snuggled against him, her hand, flat on his chest – she could feel his heart beating there. "No, Jake. You're just fine, you really are." She kissed the back of his neck again, "You don't need to put on a show for me. Yes, all... all that, with the muscles and the huge... that was all fun, I really loved that you made an effort. But this," she held her palm tighter to his chest, "this *everyday* Jake is who I *really* love." She moved her hand and ran it gently down his side, across his hip.

"This is plenty for me."

"But–" he began.

"But nothing. I've seen it all – I peeped!" she giggled "You've got nothing to worry about."

He turned around to face her, searching her eyes, "You mean it?"

"Come on, let me show you," she whispered.

This time, they made love slowly, tenderly, meaningfully. Gone were the theatrics, the catharsis from yesterday. There was no tension or urgency, they were lost in each other. Their true selves.

Afterwards, they lay silently locked in soft, warm embrace. Then, silently, without a word, Jake simply evaporated.

Kat smiled, and slipped out of bed, "Come on dog. Down you get, lunch time."

Even with half the day gone It still seemed like forever until night time. Jake paced the apartment anxiously while dark, grey clouds returned to linger depressingly above.

"It should be clear tonight," she said. Jake dumped himself down in his soft bed, chin hanging over the edge.

"Do you think you should eat before we go out?" Kat was just trying to make conversation to pass the time. Jake huffed – she didn't know what that meant, but carried on regardless "Marcus didn't really say, did he?" she rambled, "I think you shouldn't eat. I think it'll be... quicker if you're hungry. What do you think?"

Jake looked at her mournfully, over the edge of his dog-bed, a damp tennis ball lay nearby, abandoned after Kat's attempt to cheer him up.

And so, the day dragged on, unrelenting hours stacked in front of them like blocks of concrete.

1am. Kat's torch cast a small pool of wavering light ahead of her. Behind, the canal path led back to the orange lights of the footbridge. The lights and the sounds of the town had left them quicker than she had expected, and the path she thought she knew well was suddenly uneven and dangerous.

Doing nothing all day had been exhausting. Jake had slept for most of it, as dogs do. Kat managed to sleep for a few hours in the early evening but it was a fitful sleep, haunted by dark shapes, much like the looming masses of the trees and bushes by the side of the canal now.

The sky was black, though Kat couldn't make out many stars after the glare of her torch and the moon which hung gibbous and yellow towards the west, playing in the treetops.

Jake trotted ahead, stopping from time to time to let Kat, with her poor, human vision and awkward ambling bipedal gait catch up.

This time, he stopped, sniffing the air. He looked to Kat and huffed. They were close; a hundred or so metres and they were at the style that led up to the hillside. Kat had to lift him over – boy, he was heavy. He leapt from her arms to the ground and began sniffing the grass excitedly, his tail thrust into the air. He paused, air-scenting; Kat could make out his eyes closed as he drew in the scents and signs from all around.

Suddenly, he paused a low growl building in the back of his throat. Kat swung her torch towards him and at that instant a burst of golden mist imploded into him leaving him larger, sinewy muscles shifting and sliding beneath his fur as he circled once, nose to the ground. He ended facing Kat, his eyes lifted from the ground, yellow, savage, his fur had taken on a grey, coarse look. Wolf-eyes locked with hers and his lips pulled back revealing huge white daggers, a single thread of drool catching the light of her torch.

Kat took a step backwards, ice coursing through her veins. Jake stepped forwards, growling low.

"Jake," she whispered, then a little louder, "Jake It's me, Kat." He stopped, sniffed the air again and with an unearthly howl bounded off into the darkness.

No, not this one... I am Jake... Jake! The female is mine. Protect... I hear prey, I smell them, see their trails in my mind. I see the freshness of their tracks. GO! Now! Hunt them, kill them! EAT!

Run. Run fast, run silently, keep low. I smell where they are now, smell their breath, their scents, smell the grass, bruised and tell-tale under their feet. THERE! Together. A group and their young.

Closer. Closer, low to the ground. STRIKE, RUN, CHASE, they scatter, but I see the slow ones I pick my target, a mother, one of their young. They stick together, but this is their doom, alone, I am fast, together, they are slow. The young one stumbles, abandoned now – mother, save yourself save your future young. This one is lost, lost to ME.

A broken leg. I can smell the blood, the fear before I see the shape struggling on the grass. No time to look, to think. STRIKE. The blood is hot, sweet, exciting, nourishing. The struggle is over, it is done, the light from the young one draws into me fills me, calms me.... me. me. Jake.

Kat had heard the nightmare sounds of the chase. Her torch, turned off held tightly in her trembling hand. With the moon just above the hill, the only light now was diffused through a solitary cloud, the stars blazed above, their feeble light adding nothing.

It was quiet now. Was it over? She strained her eyes to make out a dark shape loping towards her in the darkness. Those long legs weren't Jake's, they were the Wolf. She backed up, felt the wooden beams of the style behind her – nowhere to run. The Wolf stopped, a few metres away. Its muzzle and chest were dark with blood. The moon began to emerge from behind its cover, as if it had been hiding from the scenes of terror up on the hill. As if on cue, the Wolf trotted towards her, running now, leapt – and in mid air an explosion of golden mist engulfed them both. Jake collided with her, licking her face and whining while she tried to pick herself up.

"Holy crap, Jake," she hissed, still respectful of the dark of the night. "I thought I was next." She laughed, but that came out in a half-sob of relief.

Jake was sitting on the grass now, trying to lick himself clean. It was all but impossible to clean his own chest so he started on a paw that had held the lamb down... or had it slashed it; things were a little unclear to him at that point.

Kat felt the wetness on her face and smelled blood on herself. She put her hand to her cheek and pulled it away, dark in the moonlight.

"Shit." she breathed, "I didn't think about that." She looked at her hand and wiped it on the grass. "We can't walk back home through town looking like this." She looked around and spotted a blocky, low rectangle not far off. "Ah, yes come on this should do." She marched off along the sheep trail with Jake following along behind.

The water trough was full, thank goodness about knee height. She lifted Jake into the cold water and splashed it over his face and back. Next, she did the best she could to remove the blood from her own face. Some had gotten onto her jacket, but thankfully, she had chosen a dark green one. She thought to herself that dark clothing would have been a good choice, but she'd just grabbed this one randomly.

She checked her face with the camera of her phone. The image was ghastly, overexposed in the dark, with the flash. She was reminded of the iconic scene from the movie *The Blair Witch Project*. Fuck, her hair; how had blood gotten into her hair? She lifted Jake out and nearly tripped jumping back as he shook, the spray of water catching the moonlight, like a silvery version of his own golden mist.

Kat pulled off her jacket, took a breath and dunked her head into the freezing cold water. That would have to do, it really would.

Thankfully, the journey home was uneventful. At this late hour, there was nobody about, the CCTV would only see a woman walking her dog, late at night. The only people they encountered were a group of lads in a clapped-out car that roared over the crossing, not slowing. One cat-called drunkenly from the back window, the driver sounded his horn and they sped off.

When they got back to the apartment, Kat was shivering and Jake looked bedraggled. The water in the sheep trough wasn't quite as clean as she'd hoped. Bits of weed and green... something, stuck to his fur.

"Ugh, let's get cleaned up." she said. Jake huffed and wagged his soggy tail.

Kat set the shower to warm for Jake and stripped off, out of her wet clothes. They still smelled faintly of blood, plus something deeply unpleasant. Jake was worse.

"Wait there," she instructed and padded off to the kitchen, a few moments later she returned brandishing a bottle of 'no-tears' puppy shampoo. "Thought that would come in handy at some point." Jake panted, smiling a toothy, doggy grin.

There was plenty of room for them both in Jake's high-end designer shower. She lathered his fur, working it through to get it golden and clean again. She let him shake off in the shower cubicle after rinsing him off. "Pop outside while I get clean, will you?" He turned and sat outside, panting happily while Kat turned up the temperature and soaped herself over with... she squinted at the bottle through the steam Coconut and Lychee body wash. Good enough.

Satisfied and warmed, Kat stepped naked from the shower. Jake was still sitting there, panting gently, looking up at her, a little red lipstick bobbing with his breath.

Kat laughed and threw a towel over him before wrapping one around herself, "No, Jake. Bad boy – not like that."

CHAPTER 13

    Moonset: 04:29.
    Moonrise: 12:35. Set: 05:01. (80.9%)
    Sunset: 18:25.

THE EFFECTS OF sleeping half the day and hunting late into the night had given Kat hellish jet-lag. Besides, she wanted to wait until Jake turned back so that she could talk with him about whether the night's escapades had worked.

Another gulp of gone-cold coffee and she put down her book – finished. Jake lay at the foot of the bed sleeping peacefully. Sheesh, how is it that he could be sleeping after all this? Dogs, she realised had the capacify to just 'switch off', they don't have the worries of the world to keep them awake at night.

She looked at her phone. 04:25 – just another four minutes. She got out of bed and pulled Jake's fluffy white robe from the chair. It was a little chilly and he'd probably feel the cold later.

Kat sat on the edge of the bed, watching him sleep. She stroked his side slowly and he shifted slightly. As the golden mist began to draw itself from the air, Kat laid the robe over him, shifting it as his legs, body, arms stretched and expanded.

"Bloody hell, Jake." She cursed under her breath as a contented snore drifted out from the curled up shape under the robe. She considered leaving him there, but he wasn't properly covered.

"Jake?" she shook him gently, again, "Jake, you're back now. You want to get into bed, it's freezing."

He stirred, yawned and saw her leaning over him. "I think it worked," he said sleepily, "I feel so... Calm." He dropped the robe over the edge of the bed and climbed inside. The bed was cold until Kat joined him and they huddled together under the duvet.

"You certainly seem more relaxed," Kat said eventually.

"You mind if I go full-dog tomorrow? It's a bit of an effort holding shape, I'm bloody knackered after yesterday."

"Yeah, that's okay. We should go to the park again get some air." But she realised she was wasting her breath; he was asleep again.

The ball squeaked the first time it bounced, and Jake caught it on the second. He bounded happily back to Kat, tail wagging. She forced a grin, even though she really *was* happy to see Jake enjoying himself so much. She was so tired that her face felt numb.

"Good BOY Jake," she slurred as he dropped the ball at her feet and barked expectantly. Was he doing this naturally, or was he *acting* like a dog out in the park? She'd have to ask him later – if she could remember.

The early walk in the park *had* to be a good idea, right? Some fresh air, clear the head. It was working for Jake, but there was no way Kat could face work today. She pulled out her phone and dialled while Jake sat patiently panting.

"Jerome. Hi." She started, apologetically. "Look, I'm

really sorry but I feel like total crap today–"

"I know what's going on Kat, don't think I've not noticed." Jerome interrupted. A flush of cold swept through her. "Young love." His voice softened, "God knows, the pair of you need each other. Take the week off, get it out of your system." Jake was starting to get a little impatient now, eyeing the ball and exhibiting a clear case of 'tippy taps'. "It's good that you're together. Besides, we need someone to keep Jake on a tight leash – we can't have any more surprise plotlines. My heart can't take it." Kat snorted, *oh if only he knew*. She thanked him, hung up and hurled the ball. Jake tore off across the grass.

This time, Kat wasn't really looking where she was throwing and it landed near to a large German Shepherd investigating a piece of litter that had blown from somewhere. Jake skidded to a halt, a few metres from the other dog and stood stock-still.

Curiosity got the better of the larger dog and it approached the bright red ball to give it an exploratory sniff – at that instant, Jake flew through the air, barking ferociously, snapping his teeth. Startled, the big dog backed up away from the ball. Jake stared the German Shepherd down, growling, sharp, white teeth flashing in the early morning sun.

The other dog, intimidated suddenly yelped and took to his heels in search of its unseen owner.

Jake grabbed the ball and marched purposefully back to a dazed Kat.

"Jake!" she yelled, "What was that?" He dropped the ball at her feet, sidled up to her and peed against her leg. Kat jumped back, "The Fuck, Jake!"

Jake took a step back and barked once, sharply.

"Screw this, we're going home," she growled, shoving the ball into her pocket. It squeaked ridiculously as she did but she was in no laughing mood now. She clipped the lead on and stormed off back to the apartment, Jake trailing behind grumbling occasionally.

"On your bed!" she ordered furiously and stomped off to the bedroom to change.

When she returned, carrying her laptop he was glaring at her from his bed, eyes following her across the room.

A couple of minutes later, Marcus appeared on the screen. He'd read her text and agreed to talk right away.

"And there was no provocation at all?" he asked.

"No, he just snapped at the other dog. It was huge too." She went on to describe the rest of the behaviour.

"I see..." He sat back in the creaky wicker chair and rubbed the back of his neck. "This is just the kind of aggression you'd expect without correction." He stopped again, not to think, but to prepare to give Kat the bad news. "It looks like he needs to go out and make another kill. That little lamb may not have been enough – It's got to be something bigger; a grown sheep."

Jake had heard this and made a groaning sound from across the room.

"You have to go out again tonight." He concluded.

"But how can we? Surely, the farmer would have seen the mess we left behind last night. He'll be on the look out – they SHOOT dogs that kill livestock."

"Trust me." Marcus said, "We'll take care of that. Go out at two am, make the kill and lie low for a couple of days. Jake will be fine after that, I promise."

"How can you be so sure?"

"It's well documented. There have been... experiments." he said. Kat decided she didn't want to know the details anymore. So long as it worked.

After Marcus had signed off, Kat looked at Jake. He looked thoroughly depressed.

"We've got to do it, you know that?" she said.

Jake got to his feet, turned about and pulled his plush dinosaur from his bed, shook it violently and let it fly half way across the room. He huffed, circled in his bed and flopped down. That was that then.

Jake struggled and growled as Kat tried to lift him over the style. A blast of golden mist engulfed them and he seemed to double his weight. She lost her grip and he slipped over the gate and onto the grass. His fur had changed in that moment to a thick, prickly mass that startled her, and the growling had become guttural and deep. This was no longer *her* Jake.

In an instant he was gone, lost in the darkness, the thundering of his paws fading fast. If the wolf-Jake from yesterday was at all unsure, this animal was a confident killer.

As Jake raced across the field his mind was laser-focused. The cloud-covered moon shed little light on the field, but the darkness was no obstacle at all – the hill was lit as clear as day in sharp monochrome, the heat from the clumps of sleeping sheep blazed like bonfires, and their scent trails hung in the air like neon ribbons.

He was upon them before they even knew he was
coming. A ewe, heavy with twins struggled to her feet
but was knocked sprawling and scrabbling as the killing
machine cannoned silently into her tearing at her
throat. The others scattered, bleating and screaming
forgetting their young in their desperate terror. One
small one stood frozen to the ground nearby as The
Wolf completed the kill.

The taste of blood was once more hot and sweet and
familiar. The ewe spasmed and was still, only rocking
sporadically as The Wolf tore at her insides. In his vision
he saw the silvery filaments and tendrils of his prey's life
force unravel and twist in the air, sucking slowly into
his own body a thousand times as nourishing as the
flesh he was devouring.

Now, the life force had gone and the feast seemed
bland. The Wolf stopped, sniffed the air – the sheep
were long gone, even the lost lamb had wandered away
to safety. He scanned the field, then a clump of bushes
and trees a short distance away. There was a shape, the
heat from a body, low to the ground foolishly thinking
that it could hide.

He slunk towards it, body low to the ground. Half
way there now and it seemed not to have seen him in
the near pitch blackness. There was a scent. Familiar,
forbidden? Movement. He froze, body pressed into the
grass, all but invisible. Had his next target seen him?
The lust for life-force was gnawing at him, he mustn't
lose this last kill. It was big; he was certain that it would
quench the thirst.

The animal broke cover, moving clumsily. In an
instant, The Wolf sprang, silently, deadly as the shape

from the bushes rose up onto two legs and yelled.

Then it was over. The man was dead, drained and torn. Something behind the mind of The Wolf beat its fists against the backs of its eyes, screamed to be heard. "It's a man! I've killed a man!" it was saying over and over until eventually the words gained meaning and The Wolf started to realise.

It had killed a man. But the life force was so powerful and pungent and invigorating. **But I have killed a man.**

Remorse flooded through The Wolf, pushing it back, away from the bright light of reasoning, it howled long and deep and chilling in the night air. In the next breath, the sound had turned to the dog-cry of Jake lost in anguish, shrunken now, almost feeble.

From the bottom of the hill, the gruesome sounds of the sheep being devoured drifted down to Kat as she paced anxiously, wanting it to be over. When the screams of a man rang out in the blackness, she feared that Jake has been hurt.

She ran towards the sound, torch flashing and waving wildly. But then came the howl and she stumbled to a halt, eyes wide in terror. Silence – then when she finally heard the dog barks and cries, her feelings were torn. The Wolf had gone, so that had to be good, but what was the rest of the story? Things had clearly gone very badly wrong.

She called to him, "Jake! Where are you? What happened?" The darkness swallowed up her words, but then she heard Jake barking somewhere to her left. She could just about make out a small stand of trees or bushes in the cloud-covered moonlight and headed towards it.

Suddenly, Jake appeared out of the void. Her torch caught his eyes, flashing green – his face and muzzle were painted red, fur matted with gore. He barked once, turned and ran back towards the shadows of the trees.

Kat set off after him, picking her way through the darkness. She passed the remains of the sheep, strewn across the grass and steaming slightly in the cold air. Kat gagged at the site and the smell that now assaulted her, turned her head away and pressed on.

When she caught up to him, he was standing over a body whining desperately. Kat's breath caught at the sight of the man, clearly dead laying on his back. He was a large man, his clothes were torn and the white skin of his belly glistened in the torch-light. Slowly, Kat approached the body, his chest and neck were soaked in blood – then she saw his face and her head swam. She knew this man. It was Jake's neighbour – 'Poirot'.

The man was dead and she didn't even know his real name. But what in God's name was he doing out here, in the middle of the night.

"Oh, Jake. What's happened?" was all she could manage to say. Jake took a step towards her, his ears were pinned back. "Why was he here? Has he been following us?"

Jake shook his head, slowly. It was strange to see such a human expression.

Just then, Kat's phone chimed startling them both. It was Marcus.

[Marcus] How did it go? Did you get what you needed.

Marcus was being guarded with his language, but there was no time for that. Kat typed back.

[KAT] Theres a dead man Jake killed someone

There was a pause, then.

[Marcus] I see. Go home now, go home and stay there.
[KAT] But what aou the man???
[Marcus] Just go. We'll take care of everything. I'll come see you at noon. Just stay in the house. Sleep, both of you.

Kat made a frustrated screen. "Fuck you, Marcus – how can we sleep after this!" She stepped back and her foot touched something in the grass. It was a set of keys, *Poirot's* keys. She picked them up and saw the Chihuahua key chain. "Shit." She tried to compose herself, "Jake. Marcus wants us to leave now, go home and wait for him. I've no idea what's going to happen now."

As it happened, sleep was not a problem. After showering, it seemed to take forever to get Jake dry with a hair drier. He nodded off several times before they were finished. Too tired even to find her pyjamas, Kat curled up in bed with Jake. His soft, clean fur felt wonderfully warm against her skin and before she knew it she was fast asleep.

Thursday 25-March-2021.

  Moonset: 05:01.
  Moonrise: 13:53. Set: 05:26 (88.9%)
  Sunrise: 05:55. Sunset: 18:26.

Some time later she woke briefly – a sound, a movement perhaps. Jake was back in human form sleeping peacefully. She pulled herself closer to him, kissed the back of his neck and drifted off once more.

"There's got to be something" Jake was pacing in the kitchen, the large coffee mug trembling slightly in his hands.

"No, nothing on the BBC news." Kat tapped a couple of times on her phone "Maybe nobody's found him yet."

"I doubt it, it's nearly eleven. I could smell dozens of other dogs up on that hill, someone would have been out walking their dog and found him by now."

"Even with the sheep there? Maybe nobody's up there because of the sheep?" Kat reasoned.

"No, there was very recent scent." He took a swallow of coffee. His hands were shaking.

"Shit... I found something." She stopped to read, muttering under her breath, "No! This is impossible!"

"What? What does it say?" Jake leapt round the other side of the island to peer at Kat's phone. She read the article out loud.

"Unidentified male, discovered dead... Yes, dog walker, early in the morning... Parker's Hill, Wednesday 24th March. Police treating as – get this –

unexplained, but not suspicious! What the hell?"

Jake put his hands up to the sides of his head and clenched his eyes shut. "How? How is being torn to bloody shreds not suspicious?"

"Marcus said he'd take care of things. Is this what he meant? Can they really do this?"

"They must have a lot of influence to make this kind of thing go away." said Jake shaking his head slowly.

Kat was looking very pale now.

"You okay?" Jake asked.

Kat put her palm up, "Yeah, just feeling a bit– No. Not okay–" She dashed off to the bathroom and slammed the door. Jake followed and heard her retching. When she came out, Jake held her. She put her head on his shoulder.

"Sorry, just the shock of hearing the news, I guess." She said quietly. Jake held her tighter, drew in the scent of her hair.

"Yes." He replied flatly, "Yes, it's probably just that."

She opened her eyes and saw the set of keys on the bedside table. They had left a small smear of blood there.

"Look." she gasped, "*Poirot's* keys. I must have picked them up last night." She pulled away and went to pick up the stained keys. "There's something very funny about that guy. Why on earth was he up on Parker's Hill last night?"

"Stalking you? I wouldn't put it past him." said Jake with a sneer, "He always looked like a proper perv." He laughed coldly, "Think I'd have torn his throat out, Wolf or no Wolf."

"We should go down and check out his apartment."

Kat suggested.

"Seriously?" Jake scoffed, "I know I might sound a little like him at times, but this isn't a bloody Scooby Doo cartoon."

Kat tossed the keys up in the air and caught them, "No, you're more like Shaggy." She marched off, "Come on then," she called behind her.

"And what? You're Daphne then?" he called after her pulling on his trainers.

"No..." came her voice from the hallway, fading fast. "Velma!"

"She doesn't even *wear* glasses," Jake muttered to himself dashing to catch up.

"How come the hallway seems longer than yours?" Kat asked after they had stepped out of the lift. The passage looked almost identical to the one above, but yes it did seem longer. Jake strode ahead.

"Um. I guess his apartment runs under my terrace, the lower floors just have balconies." The thick carpet deadened their voices.

"Oh. I didn't know there was a difference," Kat was impressed. They reached the end of the passage and stood for a few moments, looking at each other. Kat held up the key. "Wait." She stopped and fished around in her hoodie pocket. She pulled out two pairs of pink marigolds and gave a pair to Jake.

"I have too many questions," said Jake dryly.

"Fingerprints. They were under your bathroom sink and I had them since last night." She rattled off.

Jake shrugged and took the proffered gloves. He tried to snap one at his wrist like a surgeon's glove but it was too floppy.

The door opened smoothly and they braced themselves for an onslaught of yapping from the little dog Foufou... nothing.

It was dark inside with the heavy living room curtains closed. Eerie too because the layout was essentially the same as Jake's; perhaps the living room was a little shorter.

Kat sniffed. The air was musty, like nobody had lived there for months – but there was something else, something– "Smells like someone died in here." Jake said, breaking the silence.

"Yeah," Kat kept her voice low, "that's what I thought. Come on, let's look in the spare bedroom. It'll just be him here. I bet he keeps it as a study."

The blackout curtains in there were closed too. Just a little light leaked through the small window and splashed onto the carpeted floor. Jake switched on the light, his breath caught.

"Wow," he breathed, "he's been busy." The room was empty except for a desk, a single chair and a low filing cabinet upon which a plant of some kind had died a long and unhappy death.

But what caught their attention was the wall behind the desk. Virtually the entire surface had been covered with neatly arranged photographs, sticky-notes, pieces of paper with carefully written notes stuck on with tape or blu-tack.

A large section, maybe over a third of the space was dedicated to covert photographs of Kat on her way to or from Jake's apartment. One seemed to have been taken from a camera hidden in the plant pot at the end of Jake's lobby. There was a bundle of pages skewered on a nail that had been thrust into the wall. They appeared to have been a log of Kat's comings and goings.

She shuddered, peering at a colour print from last summer, she had on shorts and was carrying the obligatory coffee cup. "What kind of a perv was he?" she growled. "I mean, look – he's been stalking me for nearly a year by the looks of it."

"Hey, what's this? I don't recognise this place." Jake had pulled a badly exposed still from a video, complete with time-stamp from the wall.

"Motherfucker! That's my old apartment! How the hell did he manage that?" her fists were balled, and she tried to pace in the enclosed space, but it was no good.

Jake turned the photo over. "Broadband engineer. June something 2020"

She stopped for a moment, brain churning, then realisation dawned, "The fucker! That was him! He was wearing a facemask, but now I think of it, yes. The sicko was in my apartment."

"Oh." Jake held a handful of pages that he'd picked up from the desk, "This paints an even darker picture." he handed them over to Kat with a grim expression.

She leafed through them. Floor plans of her apartment block, a red felt-tip circle marking the kitchen of Mr Preston's empty flat, a photo of the burned building. The papers dropped to the floor as her hand went limp.

She was shaking with rage now. Jake pulled her close and stroked her hair, hoping to calm her.

"I feel sick. What was he after? Why did he DO that?" She put her head on Jake's chest and tried to breathe slowly.

"Let me get you a glass of water or something," Jake offered.

"No, I'll go get it. I've got to get out of here." and she left, for the kitchen.

"I'll see if I can figure out what he was up to." He called after her.

The kitchen was done out in what looked like antique oak or something. Kat thought the dark wood made it feel gloomy, like the rest of the apartment. She found a mug, peered into it dubiously and filled it from the water dispenser on the fridge... one of the fridges. She gulped the chilled water. Why on Earth would he have *two* huge American style fridges? Curiosity got the better of her and she opened the one without the water dispenser.

The mug smashed on the tiled floor as Kat recoiled in horror. There, on the middle shelf enclosed in a large ziploc bag the bulbous and very dead eyes of the murdering creep they called *Poirot's* tiny dog stared out at her.

She lurched to the sink as Jake came running into the room and vomited. Jake held her as she retched dryly a few times.

"What's *wrong* with this guy?" she croaked, spitting into the sink and rinsing her breakfast away. She took a handful of water and spat it out into the sink as Jake gingerly closed the fridge door.

"That's pretty fucked up," he admitted.

Just then, there were voices at the door. Indistinct,

but they were definitely just outside. The pair looked at each other in horror. "Quick," Jake hissed, and dragged Kat by the arm to the bedroom. The bed was large and they dove under just as the sound of a key in the lock could be heard.

The voices again, purposeful, organised. Several people entered the apartment, a man barked orders.

The Police?

"Shit. They've come to search his apartment." Kat whispered, hardly daring to breathe. Jake motioned her to silence as the bedroom door burst open. Footsteps, then a pair of sandals appeared beneath frayed jeans. This wasn't the police. The feet stopped next to the bed, Kat's heart was in her throat, Jake had completely frozen.

"Really? You taking the Mick?" the voice called out, "Is that the best hiding place you can think of? Come on, out you come, both of you." A face appeared right in front of them under the bed.

Jake yelped. "Marcus?" The faux mystic held out a hand to help pull him out.

"Didn't recognise your voice." Kat mumbled, sliding out from under the bed.

"Oi! Colin," Marcus called out to the living room in his real east-end accent, "Go get Miriam. Pronto."

"Look, Marcus." Jake squared up to the man. He was wiry, but a good head taller than Jake, "What's going on here?"

"What, apart from you guys breaking into the home of my dear departed operative?" he began with a sneer. "Clean-up squad. The lads here are going to make old Francis here vanish into the wind."

"Francis?" began Kat, a sad tone to her voice, "That was his name?" Then she remembered, "What the hell was he up to? Spying on me, arson, murder, he bloody killed his dog and shoved it in the fridge, did you know that?" she seethed.

"Oh, you've met Foufou?" he laughed, "Yeah, he's had that stupid dead dog for nearly ten years now."

Kat gawped, this wasn't making sense. Marcus explained, "He's a necromancer," he said the word like it left a foul taste in his mouth, "warms it up when he needs it for cover or something."

"Necro–?" Kat began.

"Foufou's a zombie Chihuahua." Jake intoned flatly.

"That's the chap, yes. Never really was comfortable with necromancy. Unnatural, like." Marcus said. "But yeah, Old Francis was supposed to be watching you, keeping you safe. He had to check you out Kat, make sure that you could be trusted, make sure you were *right* for Jake.

"But he ballsed it up, got himself killed – pillock!"

A woman in a dark blue boiler-suit and round bottle glasses peered around the door "You needed me, Mr Felton?"

"Ah, yes. Can you take Jake here and get a blood sample? Test it for second-stage lycanthropy, let me know ASAP." He nodded to Jake to go with the woman.

Jake looked at Kat, she nodded. "Um, okay. Be right back then." he said uncertainly.

"I brought something for you," Marcus said when Jake had gone. "I was hoping to get you by yourself some time this morning."

Kat inclined her head quizzically, "Oh?"

He opened a small rucksack that had been hanging from his shoulder. He quietly pushed the door closed and turned to Kat; he had a clear plastic bag in his hand, something light yellow lay inside.

"I need you to be safe." he began, offering Kat the bag. She took it, "But don't open it just yet."

"Looks like a plastic spud-gun." she said, grinning. "This isn't going to be a lot of good against a mugger."

"It's not for muggers." Marcus said sombrely.

The penny dropped. "It's for Jake, isn't it?" she said. Marcus nodded slowly, "This is to protect myself against The Wolf." Kat continued, flatly.

"It is. At this stage, we just don't know which way things are going to swing. Killing Francis may have undone all the benefit that we got from the sheep."

"No, no, no. I can't do this. I can't kill Jake!" she hissed, trying her best not to scream at him. "What do you think I am? Can't you just look after him until you know for sure?" she asked, "Like, quarantine him?"

"That doesn't work. We've tried it before. Something about the stress of confinement precipitates The Wolf in almost every case we've studied. And it's usually irreversible in those conditions."

"So, am I in danger?" she said, looking at the strange gun with unconcealed disgust.

"Less so than most." He sat on the bed. "The Wolf will often attack strangers, so if we were to provide support to stay with you, then nobody will be safe. Almost always, The Wolf will seek to protect those that they're close to. You're the best option."

"Almost always?" she repeated. "I'm not sure those

sound like good odds."

"It's the best we have." he said sadly. "Look, he's clearly stuck on you. He'll do everything in his power to keep you safe."

Kat felt cold inside. Her stomach churned. "So how does this work? Like, if I *need* it?"

"Obviously, this is one of those last stand kind of things, but you just point and shoot. You only get one shot though. It's a 3D printed cellulose polymer. It'll dissolve in water, gone in minutes in hot water if you need to dispose of it fast – even the bullet. That's a silver-impregnated polymer." He almost sounded proud of the weapon, "Quite revolutionary, but not something we want to get into the wrong hands. So DO drop it in a mug of coffee if you're found out!"

Kat turned the bag around in her hands and noticed a little sachet in there. Marcus saw her eyeing it. "Silica gel. Keep it in the bag until you need it. Moisture in the air would start to weaken it."

Jake's voice could be heard approaching; Kat stuffed the bag in her hoodie pocket and Marcus jumped to his feet.

Kat leapt to Jake as he entered the room, flung her arms around him and held him tightly. She cast a hateful glare over Jake's shoulders at Marcus.

"I wasn't gone for long." He joked, "But look at my arm!" He pushed the sleeve of his sweat-shirt up to reveal a plaster barely concealing an angry looking bruise. He turned to Marcus, "I thought you said there was no such thing as vampires!"

On their way out, they saw the 'clean-up team' dressed

in removal firm overalls busily packing up everything in the apartment. A pair were about to exit with a sofa but hung back to let Kat and Jake leave first. Kat thought she recognised the man holding one end of the sofa – was that Officer Rust? He pulled his cap down and wordlessly gestured for them to leave ahead of them.

Kat threw herself face first onto the couch when they got back.

"What time you changing today?" Came a muffled query.

"Uh, just before two, I think." Jake checked his phone, "Yeah, one fifty-three. You want to get some lunch before that?"

Kat turned over with a grunt, rubbing her belly. "I guess so. Sure." She groaned. "I think all this stress is giving me an ulcer, I feel like crap."

"Well, you did puke at *Poi–* I mean *Francis'* place. You still feeling dodgy?"

"Yeah, but who wouldn't throw up after seeing what he had in the fridge." She turned on her side, perhaps that might help. "You want me to go out and get something?"

"Would you? Anything you like, your choice." He smiled and kissed her forehead.

"You know what, I've got a hankering for sushi. That new place isn't far." The thought of food seemed to revive her a little.

"You're an angel, you really are." Jake said, fetching his wallet, "My shout of course."

Kat grinned and took the card from him, stroking

his hand as she did so.

When Kat bustled in through the door with a big paper carrier bag, Jake was just finishing a video call. The man on the other end sounded a little posh.

"–the papers drawn up right away and biked to you for signature by late this afternoon." The man concluded.

"Perfect." Jake said, looking over his shoulder at Kat. "Thanks for doing that at such short notice. Send me your invoice and I'll wire you the money right away."

"Appreciated." The man said, and they ended the call. Jake closed his laptop and stood up to greet Kat.

"That sounded official." she said, kissing him on the cheek and setting the bag down on the coffee table.

"Yuh, just some boring legal stuff." He peered into the bag "Ooh, is that miso soup?"

"Yeah, I kind of wanted something really salty. Got some for you too." She paused, "Jake?" she asked, "Can you try to do human form today. I think I need to have you about." She sat on the couch, one knee drawn up. "I really feel drained." She leant against him and let out a long breath.

Jake put an arm around her and held her. "I know, I get it. It's been pretty crazy – I'm sorry you've been through all that." He leaned forward and pulled out a waxed cardboard tub, then a second one.

"Here, don't let your soup get cold." He set it down in front of her and continued rummaging about in the bag. A good sized tray of sushi – California rolls, nigiri. "Didn't they pack any spoons for the soup?" He asked.

"No." Kat opened the tub and sniffed. "Asked them not to. Too much throw-away plastic."

He patted her on the knee and smiled, "Clever girl – I'll get some proper china ones." He went to the kitchen humming happily. Kat heard a drawer open, close then a little tinkle of breaking china.

"GODDAMIT!" Jake yelled. In that instant a blast of golden mist erupted, some even formed and sucked inwards from the kitchen door. The silence continued for a second, then a low growl which cut short. The mist blasted out from the kitchen again and Jake groaned.

Kat remembered the bag with the gun in her pocket. *I don't want this*. She said to herself and shoved it down the back of the couch. She ran to the kitchen to find Jake picking up the pieces of shattered spoon.

"Are you okay?"

Jake was shaken, "Yes. Yes, thanks I'm fine. I've got it." Kat ran across the kitchen and pulled him to his feet and hugged him as tightly as she could.

"Marcus told me that I was the only one that could be with you, the only one that would be safe." There were tears in her eyes now, "If I hold you like this, forever, you'll be fine. The Wolf won't – it won't ever come." She was sobbing gently now. "He told me something else..."

Jake ran his hand through her hair, "Shhhh." he soothed, "It's okay. It's all going to be okay."

CHAPTER 14

Friday 26-March 2021.

Moonset: 05:26.

Moonrise: 15:15. Set: 05:47 (95.1%)

Sunrise: 05:53. Sunset: 18:28.

KAT WOKE, AWARE of a weight pressing down on her body. She felt hot breath slowly blow across her face. She tried to shift, but she was pinned down by his weight.

"Hey. Saucy, haven't you had enough, we already–" a drip, on her face. "Ugh, Jake you're drooling. Really, you're insatiable." Then she saw the teeth. It was dark, but the huge white fangs caught the little light there was in the room. Now the outline of the head, black, almost on black, looming over her, the muzzle moved a little closer to her face and a glint of yellow in the eye. She felt the short prickly fur against her skin now.

"Jake." she croaked, fear throttling her, "Please."

The Wolf stopped. The hot gusts on her face ceased for a moment. Suddenly, he exploded from the bed, sending the duvet flying. Kat caught the misshapen half-human form in the darkness as it bounded towards the door, smashed against it and fumbled clumsily with the handle, its clawed hands scratching and scrabbling with something designed purely for human hands. The door flew open with a crash.

Kat leapt from the bed and threw on her sweatpants and hoodie to the sounds of things being thrown about in the living room. She had to go after him, to calm him back to his proper form. She was the only one, it was up to her. Kat turned on the bedside lamp, she didn't want to switch on the living room light for fear of startling the creature in there.

The crashing stopped and it was now making a low moaning sound. She stepped carefully into the living room, the light spilling from the bedroom was enough to make out the destruction. The coffee table was overturned and the couch seemed to have been shredded and upended.

"Jake." she said softly, though she couldn't see him. "Jake, it's me, Kat." A shape slowly rose up from behind the couch in the gloom. Inhuman, bulky, powerful. She could see the face now. Supremely wolf-like, yellow eyes illuminated by the light from behind Kat, its shadow monstrously magnified on the wall behind – The Wolf.

Deep, primordial fear churned and tugged inside Kat's chest. But she knew she would be safe. If not, then it could have devoured her there and then, or before while she was sleeping.

She moved towards it a little way. The Wolf flinched a little; she stopped. "It's okay, Jake." Then lower still, "It's okay." She took another step forward.

The Wolf growled briefly, then stopped, it's posture seeming to shrink a little. Then it rose again, seeming to have come to some kind of decision. It leapt, hurtling past Kat, knocking her against the frame of the kitchen doorway as it scrambled toward the apartment door. It was locked of course, but it threw itself against it with a thud, then again and once more until it burst open with a splintering sound and was gone.

Dazed from the impact and the sudden outburst, Kat took a moment to collect herself then set off after The Wolf – this wasn't Jake any more. She hopped through the ruined door, careful not to gash her bare feet on the daggers of wood that stuck out from the frame. The hydraulic door damper to the fire escape had just eased closed as she caught sight of it. She pelted down the carpeted hallway and burst through the door with a crash that rang in the concrete stairwell.

Automated lighting gave away The Wolf's progress downwards. She took chase as fast as she could, hand sliding and squeaking on the metal handrail in an effort not to tumble down the concrete steps and break her neck.

She could hear panting and growling below, then a thump as it tried to push through the door. It was probably a fire-door so needed the bar to be pressed first. The Wolf didn't have Jake's human intellect when it was running wild, and this gave Kat the opportunity to gain ground. She was one floor above when by luck or reasoning it got the door open. Seconds later, Kat reached the door, open to the street.

Kat got her bearings. To the right, the main entrance and beyond sprinting down the pavement, The Wolf. She set off after it – the slabs were icy cold, but there was no time to put on shoes. She gritted her teeth and urged herself onwards, faster.

She was about to remark to herself that it was lucky that there was no traffic at this ungodly hour when a car turned out of a side street ahead. He lunged and roared at the vehicle which swerved and sped away. The distraction was enough to allow Kat to gain a little, but she was no match for the hunting machine that raced ahead of her. As she passed the crossing, she knew now that there was only one place that The Wolf would go. The place it knew, the place where it could feed.

Thoughts flashed through Kat's mind as her legs pumped hard. Would it be a good thing for it to go to the field, kill another sheep perhaps? Maybe Jake had put that thought into its head before he was buried in primal instinct.

She was right. In the distance she could see him dart across the road and into the park. The cold air was making her lungs hurt now but she couldn't lose him. Shit! What would she do once she got to the towpath? Less than a hundred metres from the bridge it would be pitch black, she knew that his night vision was excellent, adapted for hunting at night.

The muscles in her legs were burning now as she hurled herself forwards along the spot-lit path in the park. It was black to either side with occasional pools of light from other paths that crossed the space.

It had to happen at some point. Her calf spasmed and she hopped to a halt, hissing through her teeth at the cramp. She was almost at the bridge but he would be down the bank and onto the towpath now for sure.

A scream rang out in the night. It came from near the bridge. Just then a figure lumbered up the bank from underneath the bridge, staggering and swerving as it ran. It stopped, turned and yelled something then continued on its uncertain trajectory towards her.

Kat braced herself as it closed.

"S'a ffkin wolfman!" A dosser – drunk or smacked out of his brain on something. He stopped and yelled at Kat, waving his arms wildly, "Run, ya stupid girl! Iss gonna bite yer ffec-ffekin heed off!"

Kat ignored him and limped towards the bridge. The guy hurled a parting obscenity at her and took off. He was under the bridge. She still had a chance.

The grass on the bank was slick with dew and she slipped, tumbling half-way down, sprawling onto the gravel path beside the canal. Kat lifted her head and squinted. Under the bridge, lit by the sporadic flickering of a failing sodium light was a shape. The Wolf – Jake, please let it still be Jake in there – was slumped against the wall, motionless.

"Jake." she called softly, pulling herself painfully to her feet. His head came up slowly, turned to look at her. He looked exhausted. Faint wisps of golden mist hung around him, occasionally darting in or wafting out.

"Don't... don't come any closer." He managed. His voice was a low, guttural growl.

"I want to help you, Jake." she pleaded, "We can push The Wolf back."

"I can't." He sounded defeated. The activity of the mist rose a little as he spoke and he grunted with effort. "I can't control it any more."

"We can, my love. We–"

"NO!" he yelled. Mist swirled around him and he seemed to gain mass, muscles swelling and writhing under the short grey fur. He calmed a little, taking slow, deliberate breaths. Slowly, he shrank a little and the mist subsided. "No. It's no use, it's too late." He stood, slowly. Unfolding from the gravel, a clear two head-heights taller than Kat.

It was then that she saw he had something clutched in his clawed hand.

"There's only one way forward now. I tried to say goodbye back at the flat, but I was pushed back into the darkness." His voice broke, "I had to go, I knew that if I stayed, I'd hurt you."

"But you won't." Kat stepped towards him to hold him, but he moved away, near to the edge of the black water of the canal.

"I wanted to spare you from this. I tried," He raised his hand to show the gun that Marcus had given her, "but I couldn't do it."

Kat gasped, "That's good. There's hope, let me take that." She reached out her hand, trembling from the cold, from fear, from the run.

Jake stepped towards her, his bulk looming above and placed the small gun in her hands. His claws scratched against the plastic.

"No. You don't understand." He said stepping away again. "I couldn't do it because I can't reach the trigger." He held up his hand – more paw now, dagger-like claws extending from misshapen fingers.

"I won't!" she yelled defiantly, throwing the gun behind her.

"I can't live like this and I can't live with myself if I hurt you. This is taking every ounce of my will to even speak with you right now. The Wolf is winning, pushing me away."

A swirl of mist again danced and sputtered around

Jake's body. He howled. Such a pitiful outpouring that Kat's heart was torn apart. She blinked, but the blur was from the hot tears streaming down her face.

"You have to... now, while I can still hold it." He strained. Kat couldn't speak. Then Jake lost his foothold in the battle, just for a moment. The Wolf snarled and lashed out with the back of its paw knocking Kat to the ground. The back of her head slammed against the concrete wall of the underpass and her vision swam for a moment. She blinked and rubbed the back of her head. When she looked up, The Wolf was standing over her, massive, all sinews and teeth. A thick line of drool hung from his mouth and slowly broke free as he approached.

Kat put her hands to the ground to get up and touched something. The gun. In that instant The Wolf let out a bone-chilling snarl and leapt. A sharp crack rang round the space beneath the bridge, a howl of pain through the smoke. Kat was blinded for a moment, then a tremendous splash and silence.

Kat stared in horror at the gun in her hands, a delicate whisp of smoke curling from its short, ruined muzzle. She threw it like it had bitten her. It skittered across the concrete edge of the canal and dropped into the black abyss of the water.

Jake was gone.

CHAPTER 15

Saturday 26-March 2021.

Moonrise: 15:15. Set: 05:47. (95.1%)

KAT'S PHONE RANG. She swore at it and swiped to reject without even picking it up.

It started again straight away. She yelled in frustration and was about to hurl it across the room when she saw Marcus' name on the screen.

He was probably the last person she wanted to speak with right now – he had let her down, let them both down. She accepted the call, even if just to scream at him.

"Switch on the news." he said simply.

"Whu–" she realised that she was too messed up even to speak right now.

"Just do it." and he hung up. She looked at the time on her phone. It was just coming up to twenty past noon. She rolled off the bed, still clothed, dusty, hair plastered to her face from tears.

Stumbling into the living room, she switched on the TV as the national news was handing over to the local news.

"Today, fans of the popular comic book series *The Rising Dead* mourn the death of its creator Jake Mayer who was found dead today in his home in Oxfordshire. He had suffered a short illness and lived alone. Mr Mayer is less well known as the creator of the hugely popular character *Princess Sparkes* much loved by children here and as far afield as Japan where the tales of the unicorn have attained cult status." the screen cut to enormous queues of fans in Japan waiting in line to buy the latest merchandise. "A representative of his publisher Jerome Baker told us 'Jake was a true genius, a gentle and kind soul. He was also a very private person, so the news of his passing was a complete shock to us all. We didn't even know he was ill.'" The screen cut to a bad photo of Jake, "Jake Mayer, who died today."

Kat collapsed on the couch as the news reader told of an armed robbery in the centre of town in the small hours of the morning by a man in a wolf mask. The picture cut to a spokesperson from the police, who reassured listeners that the offender was in custody and the gunshot that was reported in the night was from a starter pistol which they recovered when he was apprehended. She scoffed at the TV and switched it off. She wasn't even surprised that the police woman on the screen was Detective Poole.

"Fuck you, Marcus!" she screamed, "Fuck the lot of you! You've made everything a lie!" She pushed her face into a pillow and yelled long and hard until all that was left in her were silent sobs.

The remainder of the day was a blur. Kat drifted about the apartment like a ghost. She felt a little better after a shower, some dried blood at the back of her head gave her a start as she saw the red swirling down the drain. The injury seemed superficial and hardly hurt. But her heart was dead.

She had killed Jake. He was dead and nobody would

be coming for her – Marcus had seen to that. There would be no justice, no punishment, save for the torture that she would have to live with for the rest of her life knowing what she had done.

The doorbell chimed. Kat stood in the living room, looking towards the splintered door which she'd propped back crookedly in the frame. She remained inert, unable to motivate herself to answer it. It rang again and she shuffled towards the door, hair dripping still from the shower, wetting her sweat-shirt.

Kat's blank expression didn't change when she lifted the door aside to reveal Marcus – Of course. Who else would it be?

"How did you get up here?" she asked flatly.

Marcus held up a plastic key card. Probably Francis' door card. She didn't wait for him to ask to come in, but turned and walked away, letting him in by himself. She didn't care any more.

Two overalled operatives that had hung back in the corridor immediately went to work replacing the door. A neighbour, popped their head out from their apartment, saw the two workmen and disappeared again.

"Shall we sit?" he asked softly, using his fake accent. Kat remained standing, but motioned with her hand towards the couch. He took up the offer and sat on the couch, deliberately leaving space for her to join him.

"Kat. Let me just say how sorry I–"

"Just get to the point," she murmured.

"Yes. Okay," He took a breath, "Look, we need one more thing from you, something vitally important."

He waited for Kat to interject, to shout, but she was just standing there, pale, spots of water from her hair beginning to collect on the floor around her bare feet.

"You can't tell anyone about Jake's condition." he said simply.

Kat scoffed, "Why should I do *anything* you ask me?"

Marcus kept his cool, "There are others out there to protect. The world just isn't prepared for those like Jake – it never has been and it never will be.

"We've been doing this for over a thousand years now. It's been tough, and it's getting tougher." He pulled his phone from out of his pocket and waved it, "Imagine if we weren't able to suppress the truth about Supernaturals. Imagine the witch-hunts from the middle-ages in today's online society." He shrugged hopelessly, "it would be a massacre."

"But you just stood back and did nothing!" Kat yelled, "You just let me kill him and you did nothing to help, I was all on my own!"

"Kat. Please believe me, there was nothing we could have done. Jake was lost – and no, you have *never* been alone. You think that guy under the bridge was a homeless guy? We're *everywhere* Kat. We have a *millennia* of experience behind us."

That was a sobering thought, Kat was starting to realise how deep she was in all this now. "So, what stops me or anyone else just going to the press, or posting online?"

Marcus nodded quietly, "Imagine if you did. If you came out about your 'werewolf boyfriend'... you'd be ridiculed. We do that all the time, remember. But please. Think of Jake's reputation, his legacy. In life, he died nobly and heroically. We constructed a brave and apt death story for him. People will remember and respect him for his strength. Rather than some 'loony scandal' on the internet."

"But it just doesn't seem fair." Kat sighed.

"The world isn't fair, and people are cruel and judgemental and fearful." Marcus said with true sadness in his voice, "I know you loved him, but people can't even accept love between *humans* if it doesn't conform to their own set of ideals."

That last statement hit Kat hard. There was a deep truth in that. She sat slowly on the couch and looked Marcus in the eye.

"I think I understand now." she said.

Sunday was a dislocated mess. The clocks had gone forward an hour. She had no idea – it took her half the morning to realise why the clock in the kitchen was suddenly not the same as the one on her phone. She suspected Marcus and his goons of playing some kind of mind game.

She picked up her phone again. It was full of missed calls and messages that she had been avoiding since she woke yesterday.

There were some from Jerome – she felt she could stomach those. The first ones were his reaction to hearing that Jake had died. What had happened? Was she okay? Then slight indignation that someone from the TV had called to ask him questions. Eventually he had just left a final message

[Jerome B] Kat. I know you must be torn apart. I'll leave

The little kiss made her smile. He was a good guy when it came down to it. She decided that she would drop in to work on Monday to see Jerome.

Monday 29-March 2021.

Moonrise: 20:34. Set: 07:43 (99.8%)
Sunset: 19:33.

A RESPECTFUL HUSH swept across the office floor
when Kat appeared at the door. The news was clearly
out that Kat and Jake were an item. Mario stood at
his desk as she passed and sombrely doffed his black
goth-style *Princess Sparkles* cap. He was never seen
without it and Kat noticed with amusement that the
new girl raised an eyebrow on seeing his bald head for
the first time.

She headed straight for Jerome's office – the door
opened before she got there and he quietly ushered
her in.

"Sit, sit." He urged, offering her a place on the big
red leather couch. "You want a coffee?"

She shook her head silently

Jerome opened a desk drawer and pulled out a
bottle. "Something stronger perhaps? I know it's only
Monday morning but under the–"

"Hell yes." Kat answered decisively.

Jerome relaxed a little "I'm glad you said that, I need
it too." He poured a generous slug of scotch into a pair
of chunky tumblers. Kat accepted the proffered glass,
it reminded her of the one that Harrison Ford drank
from in the movie *Blade Runner*. They clinked classes.
"To Jake," they toasted.

"It's really hard to know what to say," Jerome began
after a sizeable gulp, "other than I'm sorry. Honestly,
I didn't even know he was ill." He tried to cover his

breaking voice with the glass.

"Yes." Kat prepared herself to deliver the lie, "It wasn't something that he wanted to share."

"Were you... Sorry I shouldn't pry..." Kat dismissed his concern with a wave, she was in it now, "Were you there with him at the end?"

Kat wasn't prepared for that one. Her hand started to shake and she had to hold the glass with both hands. "Yes," she choked. "Yes, I was there."

Jerome took that as a cue not to ask too much more. There was a short awkward silence, Kat sipped her whiskey – it tasted expensive. That was something she had learned from Jake's 'irresponsibly expensive' collection of bottles.

She noticed the portfolio on the large reading table. It was unopened. She nodded towards it, "Did you ever get to see the sketches for the new series?"

Jerome shook his head, looking at the large leather folder as if for the first time, "No. I've not even opened it since the meeting. Is it any good– yes, of course it'll be good." He got up and started opening the long zip that ran around it. He gasped and turned to Kat. Instead of the expected handful of sheets, it was stuffed to bursting. "What–"

Kat joined him at the table as Jerome started pulling out sheet after sheet of beautifully drawn, finished artwork. "This must be–" Kat began.

"–the *complete* final series." He spoke over her in hushed tones more appropriate for having discovered a Holy relic. "It's all here, it's *perfect*," he whispered, leafing through the pages, then. "Oh. Oh wow, look." He carefully lifted a sheet out for Kat to see. "The final page, look."

There, a full page pane depicting Michelle, finally dead and at peace, below it a few lines of text.

Dedicated to Kat.
My love, my inspiration, my saviour.
You showed me life, you brought me peace.

As one, they burst into uncontrollable tears. Jerome staggered to his desk and slumped face down sobbing quietly.

Kat, by now a little more used to the insane rollercoaster of life recovered first. She had the presence of mind to put the paper down on the desk and step away, lest it be drenched in tears and snot. Not the most fitting treatment to Jake's final work. She wiped her face on her sleeve then Jerome handed her a box of tissues to do the job properly.

"Quite something." he said, "I can't imagine how he did this so fast."

Kat was starting to tidy the papers up in case they got out of order. "He was kind of working through the night a lot towards the end." Then she realised, "Perhaps he knew the end was coming." She shivered.

"Look, what's that?" Jerome pointed to an envelope sticking out from the bottom of the pile. He pulled it out and read the front. "It's addressed to you," he said, handing it to her. "I think you should probably read that at home." Then he thought, "Where *is* home now?"

"I'm not really sure." She admitted, "I guess it would be okay to stay at Jake's for a couple of days until I can sort something out."

The letter sat neatly on the coffee table. Kat sat and stared at it. She knew that these were going to be the last words she would ever hear from Jake. She couldn't bring herself to read them, to make it final. Twice, she reached out a trembling hand and almost touched it. While that envelope remained sealed, there were still words that Jake could say to her, words in her future and not all in the past, dead and done.

She got to her feet, poured a glass of water. Drank half of it, paced the kitchen then walked quickly and resolutely, to the table, picked up the letter and opened it before she could stop herself.

The letter was dated Friday. How on earth had that gotten into the folio? It could only have been one of Marcus' goons.

She read:

My Wonderful Kat,

Sorry for the obvious cliché, but yes if you're reading this you will know that I've gone. It was clear to me that after what happened on the hill with Francis, that there was no going back. Marcus – you're going to have to trust him, please – told me what might happen once I, or rather The Wolf had tasted human flesh. That's how the legends began after all.

I know about the gun that Marcus gave you, I know what he asked you to do. I can't allow him to make you the one to do it. He knew that the time would come when if I stayed I'd hurt you.

And so did I.

If all has gone to plan, then I will have taken the gun and gone where nobody will find me. It's what a wolf or a dog will do when they know that their time has come.

Dearest, precious Kat, my time has come.

So, if you're reading this then you'll know why I had to go. I hope and pray that I haven't hurt you – I know that the hurt that you must feel runs deeper than flesh and blood and bones and I'm sorry.

Finally, I want you to live a life free from burden and worry. Everything that I have – the house, the money, the intellectual properties. They're yours now. For your future... and well, there's something that I can know as a dog that humans can't detect, maybe you already suspect it yourself go learn what I already know.

Don't feel sad for me. The last days of my life were the best a soul could live. I knew life with you, I knew love with you. You made me free.

Live your life now, and live it well.

I will love you, forever,

Jake. X

The night was cold, the sky dark and clear. Kat sat on the bench on the bridge over the canal, smiling serenely. The drama was over, but her heart was raw from the death of her true love. Now a new life was beginning. She took the small plastic stick from her pocket one more time and let the light of the full moon fall on it, faintly but clearly illuminating the little red plus sign.

THE END

Thanks for reading!
We hope you enjoyed this book. If you did then please consider leaving a review at Amazon – it would mean a lot to us all.

OTHER TITLES FROM

SCI-FI-CAFE

Available to buy in paperback and eBook from
Amazon and other good online stores.
Scan the affiliate links in the QR codes to find out
more about each book.

The Threads Which Bind us

Anna's life is falling apart. She's skipping college, lost touch with her friends and can't face her family. She wakes late to find the ghost of a young man in her room. He has no memory of his past life nor any clue as to why he has appeared here.

In the beginning, she fights to get rid of him, but something about his glasslike sensuality fascinates her as he is drawn towards the only person in his world that can hear him, see him, *touch* him.

As they work to find out who he is, how he died and what is keeping him in the realm of the living, Anna's own recent and tragic past surfaces.

Content advisory: Mild sex references, suicide references. Alcohol.

ISBN: 978-1-910779-98-9

The Girl from the Temple Ruins

A temple to the goddess Amalishah lies in the remotest wastelands of Assyria. She is their protector but to others she is known as The Monster.

The Hittite prince Artaxias visits the Palace of the Goddess to implore the temple priests to free prisoners captured from the border. He knows their fate, the appalling human sacrifice that will be made to the goddess who must feed on human blood.

Four thousand years have eroded the memory and the evidence of these events until British archaeologist Michael Townsend discovers the subterranean lair of the goddess. Michael is visited and instantly captivated by a mysterious and beautiful woman. The Hittites called her monster, a creature now called vampire.

ISBN: 978-1910779-41-5

City of Storms

When top foreign correspondent Sean Brian flies into Manila in the Philippines, a typhoon and a political revolution are uppermost in his thoughts.

But what also awaits will turn his already busy life into a roller coaster of romance, adventure, elation and despair.

At the centre of this transformation is an infant boy child, born, abandoned and plunged into street poverty in the grim underbelly of an Asian metropolis.

This is the catalyst for a story ranging from the corrupt, violent world of back street city sex clubs and drug addiction, to the clean air of the Sulu Sea and the South Pacific; from the calm safety of an island paradise to the violent guerilla world of the notorious Golden Triangle and the southern Philippines archipelago.

As we follow the child, Bagyo, into fledgling manhood, we can only wonder at the ripples that spread from one individual to engulf so many others – and at the injustice that still corrodes life on the mean streets of the world.

ISBN: 978-1908387-99-8

www.ingramcontent.com/pod-product-compliance
Lightning Source LLC
Chambersburg PA
CBHW030759190726
48285CB00003B/934

9 781910 779972